PSYCHOGEIST

PSYCHOGEIST
L. P. Davies

1967

DOUBLEDAY & COMPANY, INC.
GARDEN CITY, NEW YORK

All of the characters in this book
are fictitious, and any resemblance
to actual persons, living or dead,
is purely coincidental.

1

There were things that had to be done before he undressed and climbed between the cool sheets, precautions that had to be taken against the coming night, a routine that had to be followed. Edward Garvey went about his self-imposed routine with a meticulous care, not hurrying, for haste might mean oversight.

The wardrobe first, and great care had to be taken here, for a wardrobe such as this, a huge, Victorian mahogany mausoleum that dwarfed the rest of the furniture, was the place where danger might most likely lurk. He pushed aside the clothes hanging there, the few clothes he possessed, to peer first into one side, then the other. Crouching, he explored the dark corners behind dusty shoes. He reached up to the shelf to push boxes aside. Closing the door he carefully locked it and slipped the key beneath the pillow on the bed.

Then the bed, under the bed, on his hands and knees, making sure there was nothing there. And then the space behind the chest of drawers that was set at an angle across one corner of the small room.

The bedroom door next. But first a cautious silent step out on to the narrow landing, looking down the stairs into the hall, listening, mentally identifying and tabulating the soft sounds of movement from below, sounds that were an everyday part of his life, but none the less dangerous for being familiar. He closed and locked the bedroom door, and a second key joined the first under the pillow.

And finally the window. It was closed, it always was closed, whatever the time of year, whatever the weather. He inspected the catch, ran his fingers slowly round the edges where glass met perished putty.

The garden below, the tiny front garden with its row of stocks, the strip of crazy paving leading to the white-painted wooden gate, was empty. The pocket-handkerchief patch of lawn was dry and yellowed after a month without rain. Beyond the neatly-trimmed privet hedge the dusty lane was empty. Garvey stood to one side of the window, his face pressing the lace curtain against the cold glass. From here, by straining, he could just make out the fence of Milton's cottage. And Milton himself, leaning over his gate, staring away into the distance, face brown against the white of his shirt, smoke drifting from his pipe.

Behind the cottage, behind the sloping green oblongs to fields, the sun was reaching down a cloudless sky to touch the hills. But sunset was still some time away, for this was July and nine o'clock.

For a few minutes, secure behind the curtain, Garvey watched the retired schoolmaster enjoying the evening. There was no vicarious pleasure for him at the sight of the other's placid enjoyment. There was no pleasure at all in life, only danger, danger that waited in every dark corner, in every quiet place.

He undressed himself slowly, folding the discarded clothing, and climbed into bed. The glass of water that stood on the bedside table he had brought himself from the bathroom, running the water for a long time, holding the brimming glass up to the light to make sure it contained no obvious impurities. The supper he had eaten he had prepared himself, refusing, as always, his niece's proffered assistance. The breakfast he would eat tomorrow morning he would cook himself over the tiny gas stove.

Garvey sighed and closed his eyes. For a while his mind, as usual a place of tumbling, drifting thoughts, refused to let him sleep. He drifted in the twilight world that was half-way between sleep and awareness.

And in the room below, the small, bright front room with its tiny diamond-paned windows, a girl stared with horror-filled eyes at the scattered blue wreckage on the floor, her hand pressed tightly against her open mouth.

A little way down the lane, Harvey Milton, retired schoolmaster, straightened, knocked his pipe out against the gate, yawned and turned to go indoors. There was a programme on television that he particularly wanted to see. Half-way along the path he paused, frowning a little and turning to glance in the direction of the cottage on the other side of the lane. He looked up at the window of the bedroom where Edward Garvey still hovered between sleeping and waking.

Milton knew something of what had been happening in that cottage. He felt very sorry for Martha Metcalfe, Garvey's widowed sister. He felt sorry too for Rosemary, Martha's daughter, who had come to look after her uncle while her mother was in hospital. Milton wished there was something he could do to help. He tapped his teeth with the stem of his pipe, shrugged and went inside his cottage. He wondered, waiting for the set to warm up, if it would be a waste of time having another attempt at persuading Garvey to see a doctor. Not that a doctor, or even the psychiatrist who would undoubtedly be called in, would be able to do anything about the things that had been happening. But getting Garvey to see a doctor might be the first step in persuading him to leave the cottage.

Some three miles away, in the small market town of Colford, Dr. Peter Hill, who had just finished tidying the surgery after the evening's work and was looking forward to a quiet stroll before turning in, stood by the window that overlooked the tree-lined street and spent a pleasant few minutes stock-taking. Today, Saturday, marked the end of his first fortnight in Colford. In retrospect those fourteen days had been enjoyable. Already he had made friends amongst the local people. He was well on the way to carving himself out a quiet little rural rut. At thirty-two he felt it might be rather early in life to start thinking about ruts. But there is a lot to be said for them. An uneventful existence. No hurry, just a gentle drifting of the days. Peter felt certain that he was going to enjoy being in practice here. After the city, life in the country was so uncomplicated. On his way out he called to Mrs. Charnley, letting her know that he would be back for supper before ten.

Still farther away, at the other side of the country, a young man wearing a black leather jacket with a devil's head design painted on the back, skin-tight blue jeans and over-pointed shoes, with long, yellow-tawny hair curling thickly on his neck, with a filthy rucksack slung over one shoulder, stood at the side of a road and flipped a coin. After reading its message he crossed the road to take up a position facing the oncoming traffic, one arm raised, thumb sweeping arrogantly. He was lucky. Five minutes later a lorry pulled up. Without bothering to ask its destination, without proffering thanks, the young man tossed his rucksack aboard and clambered up after it. The lorry moved away in a swirl of dust and diesel fumes.

In his cottage bedroom, Edward Garvey finally fell asleep.

And on a faraway planet, a million light years away, somewhere on the dark, lonely fringes of the Galaxy, in a carvern deep in the heart of the Mountains of the Lost Moon, another man stirred and opened his eyes.

It seemed to him in the first moments of awareness that it had always been like this, that he could never awaken to full consciousness immediately, that there always had to be this hiatus of remembering, this piecing together gradually of who he was, what he was, where he was, why he was here.

His name was always the first thing he was able to remember. Dry lips—why were they so dry?—mouthed the familiar syllables. Argred. His name was Argred the Freeman. He spoke the words aloud, testing them, hearing the echo as the sound was carried away.

His head motionless—he knew that movement would mean pain —his eyes strove to pierce the semi-darkness. What light there was came from patches of blue luminosity that seemed to float against a misty grey curtain. Gradually his eyes found a focus. Now they could recognise the patches of dancing light, identify them as the Glowing Fungus that grew, clinging to the walls, that some said had come there naturally, but that others said had been developed by the Old People and set on the cavern walls to grow to light the way.

The Old People. . . .

He was in one of the caverns of the Old People. Why he was here he would be able to remember later. His hands, groping at his sides, discovered the hard rock on which he lay, his back resting against the curved wall. There were some who believed that this labyrinthian maze of tunnels and caves was natural, that the Mountains of the

Lost Moon had been so honeycombed from the beginning of time. And there were whose who said that the Old People had carved them out with wondrous, unimaginable tools.

His hands reached up to touch his face, confirming the familiarity of lean features, exploring the chiselled nose, passing over the stubble-covered jaw. That stubble—for once he had owned a beard—would be the same tawny-gold as his mane of hair. His eyes, he remembered, touching their lids, were blue. The blue of the summer sky over the surf-beaten shores of Andrida. Who had used those words? Where had he heard them before?

He knew who he was, but he still had to remember why he was here, why his body ached, why he was so tired, why his mouth was dry and his stomach hollow with emptiness. Why—and he lifted his hands again, now to peer at them in the half-light—why his hands were so painful and covered with dry, scaling blood.

His eyes were slowly learning control. Now he was able to make out his surroundings more clearly. He was lying in a tunnel carved from the grey and brown striated rock, the walls curving upwards with no boundary lines between floor and wall and ceiling. On either side the tunnel curved away into velvet blackness. The air was thin, still, dead, musty with age. There were no sounds, no silvery dropping of water. The silence was a heavy cloak. When he coughed, the breath rasping in his throat, the curved walls took up the small sound, magnifying it at first, but then carrying it away until it faded into the silence.

Argred's eyes turned upwards, the movement of his neck, small though it was, causing him to wince with pain. Somewhere above, miles above, through the miles of solid rock above his head, were the tall peaks of the mountains, tall, twisted spires thrusting into the dark blue night sky of Andrida—for it would be night up there—with its high-sailing twin moons and the crescent pattern of stars that the Mind-Healers had named the Pendant.

The Mind-Healers. . . .

Another name, another piece to add to the picture. He looked at his hands again, beginning to remember how they came to be like this, why his whole body was filled with dull pain. He had been betrayed to the Mind-Healers. Gorold, Rhoweena had told him, had

9

been the one who had betrayed his temporary hiding-place in the forest. And before that. . . .

The attack on the Palace. The smoke-red of flaming torches; the hoarse shouting; the clash of metal on metal. He had led the attack across the courtyard and it had been repulsed. The few survivors had gone into hiding. Then the soldiers had swept through the city, burning, pillaging, taking meaningful revenge. Destruction and death to teach the people a lesson they wouldn't forget.

They had come for him just before dawn. They had taken him away to one of their secret places to torture him, wanting to know the names of his confederates in the Freedom Movement. He had managed to keep silent through a day that had been an eternity of agony. How long ago had that been? Only yesterday? Here, in the bowels of the mountains there was no way of telling the passage of time, no way of telling how long he had been asleep. It was only instinct that told him it was night.

Rhoweena had found a way of rescuing him. He frowned, trying to recall the details. There had been men with her, a handful of men, Freemen of the Plains, helping in the operation not because they still needed him as their leader—for now everyone was against him, friend and enemy alike—but because they were obeying Old Lorr's orders.

Gorold, Rhoweena, Old Lorr. . . . Names as yet without faces. If he concentrated he would be able to supply faces to fit the names. But that wasn't important right now. What was important was that he remembered why he was here. There was a purpose of some kind behind his being in the caverns of the Old People. He hadn't come to seek refuge; Rhoweena had offered the sanctuary of her home. And Rhoweena was the daughter of Old Lorr, the Wise Elder of the Freemen. Even the soldiers of the Mind-Healers would think twice before violating the privacy of Old Lorr's home.

He had come to the caves because. . . .

Because there was something he had to find.

There was some thing—or was it a place?—he had to find.

A place. If it existed. If that place, and what it contained, was indeed something more than just part of a legend that had been handed down from father to son through the ages.

But he couldn't remember what was so important about that place. He couldn't remember what it was he hoped to find there. The effort of reaching back into his mind made his head spin. Leaning back against the cold stone he closed his eyes and drifted into the semi-consciousness of utter exhaustion. After a while he fell asleep again.

And in the tiny bedroom, Edward Garvey woke with a start to lie and stare at the moonlit-dappled ceiling.

He had had the dream again, the same dream that had been coming every night, and sometimes during the day, for almost a year. But as with all the other times it was already fading, slipping away from his mental efforts to hold it faster than his mind was able to collect the fragments together. Only vague impressions were left. A cave, emptiness, echoing sounds, pain, swirling mists. Then nothing. It had gone again. Only the strange sense of familiarity remained. A feeling of something that was almost nostalgia. He knew that he had dreamed of a place that was as familiar to him as his bedroom.

2

Dr. Peter Hill woke at his usual time of half past seven, spent a few moments of slow recovery gazing sleepily at the ceiling, remembered it was Sunday and turned thankfully over to close his eyes again. The smell of frying bacon woke him again at nine. He washed and shaved with the bathroom window open to the warm sunshine.

The surgery telephone rang as he was coming down the stairs, but as usual Mrs. Charnley was there to answer it, hurrying along the hall, calling up: "I'll take it, Doctor; your breakfast's out."

Seated at the table Peter was able to hear the one-sided conversation in the adjoining surgery, Mrs. Charnley's voice possessing a certain stridency.

"Beech, Upton Farm. . . . Yes, we know where that is. . . . How old is the child? When did you notice the swelling? Has there been any sickness? Yes—mumps. . . . There's a lot of it at the moment."

Helping himself to coffee Peter permitted himself a dry smile. Cook, housekeeper, receptionist, book-keeper. And for good measure, diagnostician. A woman of many parts. Uncle Andrew had her well trained. Or more likely, taking the line of least resistance, he'd just let her go her own sweet way without interference.

"Got everything you want?" enquired Mrs. Charnley from the door. In her fifties, a widow, tall and bony, she wore grey hair drawn back in a rigid bun and owned a set of brown, somewhat intimidating features with the sinister touch of a large mole on one cheek.

"Thank you," Peter told her.

"That was Upton Farm, out on the Banbury road."

"Mumps," he informed a forkful of bacon.

"I said you'd look in about eleven. You've got a visit in Padham as well. Brownlee. They called earlier. Burn. . . ." And when he looked up: "Not urgent, seemingly done yesterday. He's one of them from the Establishment. You got plenty of toast, Doctor?"

"Plenty. I thought they had their own nurse out there?"

"She don't work Sundays. Likely it's just the dressing needs changing. The address is on the pad. If you've everything you want I'll be getting about my cleaning."

Peter took his time driving out to the mumps, calling in first on Mr. Brownlee who occupied one of the semi-detached boxes on the Padham New Estate and who did indeed only require the changing of his dressing. The nurse at the Electronics Research Establishment had made a good job of the initial treatment. There had been no serum seepage and changing the lint was little more than a formality. The patient, a small, bald-headed man with the brightness of a December robin, watched the operation with interest.

"It's goin' on all right, Doc?"

"Doing very nicely. How did it happen?"

The other was frank.

"My own damned fault. Careless. . . . Solderin' iron slipped. Is it enough to keep me off, Doc?"

Closing his case, Peter grinned. "That's for your nurse to say. Far be it from me to step on her efficient toes. I've wondered—What goes on behind that formidable-looking barbed-wire fence of yours?"

Brownlee inspected the replaced dressing.

"That feels better. Don't ask me what they get up to in there. Part of a blue-print, a screwdriver an' a solderin' iron, an' that's my lot. I just do as I'm told, pay my union dues an' try to keep my nose clean. Which means keepin' it close to my own bench an' not lookin' over anyone else's shoulder."

The visit to Upton Farm was also little more than a formality, Mrs. Charnley's telephonic diagnosis being correct. Peter spent five minutes in the sick-room and the best part of an hour being shown over the farm by the garrulous father of the mumps-stricken child.

It was getting on for twelve o'clock when he arrived back at the surgery. Mrs. Charnley was waiting for him in the hall.

"Someone waiting, Doctor." And when he lifted a significant eyebrow in the direction of the grandfather clock: "She's only just come. Miss Metcalfe; she's not on our list. I think she wanted to see your uncle."

"She's got a nerve," he observed bleakly.

Mrs. Charnley sucked in disapproving lips. "She's not come about herself—her uncle. He is one of ours. I put his card out."

"I'm obliged," Peter said dryly, and went into the surgery. He read the name on the card, "Edward Garvey", and then pressed the bell.

Miss Metcalfe wore a green linen dress with white collar and cuffs. She had an oval face framed in very dark hair that sloped across her forehead and curled to her shoulders. A first-glance labelling put her as attractive, setting her age at something approaching thirty. He revised the latter part of his assessment after he had noted the shadows about her eyes and the tenseness that added artificial age-lines to a complexion which would normally have been smooth. Whoever Miss Metcalfe might be, she was seemingly suffering under some kind of strain.

She was startled to see him, but not too put out to forget to apologise for disturbing him out of surgery hours.

"We're here to be disturbed." Peter offered her a chair. "Sundays being no exception. I believe you've come about your uncle?"

She nodded. "But I was expecting to find Dr. Hill."

He smiled. "I am Dr. Hill. I imagine you were hoping to see my uncle. I'm afraid he's in hospital."

"Oh—" Her eyes widened. "I didn't know. I'm sorry."

"He's been in a fortnight. A mild heart attack. Nothing serious— he should be back in harness soon. For the record, I'm not just a ship that passes in the night. I'm here to stay. In due course I shall be taking the practice over."

"I see—" But she still sounded uneasy.

He picked up the card. "Edward Garvey. That will be your uncle?" And when she nodded: "I see he was in hospital about a year ago. Broken arm, fractured ribs and leg, extensive bruising and shock as the result of an accident. Apparently he made quite a good recovery."

"It's nothing to do with that. It's something very different. Although the accident did seem to bring it to a head. . . ."

Peter leaned back. "Hadn't you better tell me all about it?"

"It's not easy knowing where to start. . . ." She took a deep breath. "There's no real beginning. Uncle Edward is Mother's brother. Before the accident he used to work in the Gas Offices here in Colford. He never married, and he used to live in lodgings. He was very"—she hesitated over the word—"retiring. Father was about the only person he could bring himself to talk to." She paused.

"Go on," Peter encouraged gently, aware of her discomfort.

"He avoided people because he thought they were talking about him. After the accident it became worse—then he seemed to think they were trying to harm him. He used to prepare all his own meals, and he wouldn't even let his landlady into his room to clean it. Dr. Hill, your uncle, that is, knew all about him. He said it was a form of persecution mania."

Miss Metcalfe paused again, this time her raised eyebrows inviting comment.

"From your description," Peter said carefully, "it does sound like that. It would call for psychiatric treatment."

"Father and Dr. Hill between them managed to persuade him to see a London psychiatrist."

"A sensible move."

"It might have helped." She shook her head helplessly. "I don't know."

"You mean he changed his mind about going to London?"

"It was changed for him. Father arranged to travel down with him. But they never arrived. You must have read about it in the papers. The Banbury derailment."

Peter nodded. "I remember."

"Uncle Edward—well, you've got all that on his card. Father was one of those killed."

He looked down at the desk. "I'm sorry."

"Uncle Edward recovered from his injuries, although his leg and his side seem to worry him at times. But his mind became worse. It was obvious he wasn't fit to be left on his own. Mother sold her house and took a small cottage out at Betley Hatch where it's quiet.

15

Uncle Edward gave up his job and went to live with her. I had to find myself digs in Colford to be near my work in the Public Library. I was only able to get out to see Mother about once a month.

"The change didn't do Uncle Edward any good; if anything, he seemed to be worse. Mother said there were days on end when she didn't even see him. He'd lock himself in his bedroom and only come out to get himself food when she was out. I suppose it was about three months ago that I noticed it was beginning to get her down. She didn't complain, but it was obvious from her manner. Then a week ago she had a nervous breakdown and had to be admitted to hospital. I arranged my holidays so that I could go to Betley to look after things."

"And now you feel it's too much for you," Peter suggested.

She avoided his gaze. "Things can't go on the way they are. Something's got to be done before Mother comes out of hospital, otherwise the same thing will only happen again."

"I see your problem." He tugged at his ear. "Have you anything in mind?"

"I don't really know," she replied helplessly. "That's why I wanted to see your uncle. I was hoping he might have some suggestions."

And now there could be no doubt that she was refusing to meet his eyes. A flush had come to her cheeks and she moved uneasily on her chair, staring down at the tightly-clasped hands in her lap.

"Apart from anything else," she said when he stayed silent, "I feel sure that it would be for his own good if Uncle Edward could be sent to some place where he could be properly looked after."

The inevitable pay-off. He had been waiting for something like that. Peter glanced covertly at his watch—he had also been hoping for an early lunch. The interview had dragged on for nearly twenty minutes before reaching its expected climax.

He felt disappointed in Miss Metcalfe; from her appearance he wouldn't have thought she was the type. This wasn't the first time he'd had to sit through similar explanations given by people with elderly relatives who wanted those relatives put away, as they usually glibly called it, simply because for one reason or another they had become family encumbrances. He had no time for the selfishness of the thin excuse "for their own good". If people like that had it their own way the Institutions and Homes would be crammed to bursting point. An unpleasant facet of the Welfare State. . . . They pay their compulsory contributions, and in return they expect the State to take over the family obligations.

He said: "The best thing, of course, would be to persuade your uncle to see a psychiatrist. Has he ever threatened to take his own life or shown any signs of becoming violent?"

She shook her head in hasty repudiation. "Oh no!"

"So he cannot be forced into submitting to treatment. Look, Miss Metcalfe, I shall be visiting my uncle this afternoon. I'll mention it to him."

She came to her feet. "I would be most grateful, Doctor."

He opened the door for her, and she smiled for the first time as she slipped past him into the hall. It was a smile that clearly cost her an effort, and the shadows about her eyes were genuine enough. He guessed that she was sleeping badly, and felt certain that she was very worried. But if she had described her uncle's symptoms correctly, there was no cause for such obvious concern. And there was also no apparent reason why her mother, looking after a man who spent most of his time locked in a bedroom, should have suffered a nervous breakdown. There was a possibility that there was much more to this than met the eye.

After closing the outer surgery door he walked pensively back along the hall. Mrs. Charnley was waiting to tell him lunch was ready. He nodded without speaking. Instead of returning to her kitchen she followed him into the dining-room, her face alive with undisguised curiosity. But having no intention of gratifying that curiosity and adding to her store of local knowledge, he looked pointedly at the clock.

"I shall have to hurry my lunch," he told her. "I want to visit my uncle, and visiting hours start at two on a Sunday."

Peter started for the hospital a few minutes before two o'clock. He drove quickly, taking less than five minutes to cover the two miles between the surgery and the Padham outskirts. As he turned into the forecourt of the Memorial Hospital the tail-end of the flower and bag-laden visitors' queue was straggling up the main steps.

Collecting his own bag of grapes from the glove compartment he hastened in its wake.

A youth wearing a black leather jacket and dirty blue jeans sprawled his ungainly length on one of the wooden benches that edged the drive, his head resting on a rucksack, his feet on the arm of the bench. As Peter approached he thrust one leg out, barring the way, asking in an arrogant drawl: "Got a fag on you, pal?"

Peter stopped—had to stop—hesitated, felt in his pocket for his case, and when the occupant of the bench showed no sign of changing his position beyond replacing his leg on the arm, had to step forward to offer it. Three cigarettes were abstracted with long, filthy fingers and slipped without a word of gratitude into the breast pocket of the leather jacket. The youth closed his eyes. Peter grimaced and went on his way.

Dr. Andrew Hill, by virtue of a golf-club relationship with the Hospital Registrar, had been given the unwarranted privilege of a private ward on the ground floor, with french windows that gave on to a terrace graced with a view of green lawns and military beds of scarlet geraniums. Wearing a dressing-gown over his pyjamas he sat in a basket-chair in the terrace sunshine. Close-cropped white hair gave him something of a Teutonic appearance. The deep furrows of his forehead sloped to one side and were confined there, leaving the other side oddly smooth, the result of a life-time habit of raising the thick black brow of the right eye. He raised it now at sight of Peter's offering.

"Comforts for the ailing." He inspected the bag's contents. "Grapes," he discovered with little enthusiasm. "Did you remember to bring my pipe and pouch?"

"Smoking," Peter replied patiently, hoisting himself to the stone balustrade, "is out for the time being. You know that as well as I do. And how are we feeling?"

"Keep that for your patients," retorted his uncle pleasantly. "Our patients. That's if we still have any left."

Peter grinned. "Still one or two left on the list, mainly the old-stagers who came for a chat rather than attention. We've even won one or two new ones. I had to visit one this morning, one of the Establishment types. Is that the usual thing?"

"It's the usual thing." Dr. Hill selected a grape with some care and tossed it lawn-wards, in the direction of a strutting, pompous-chested pigeon. "They don't have a large enough staff to warrant a doctor of their own, so when the need arises they call on me. It's all ethical and above-board. Is that what's troubling you?"

"I didn't know it showed." Peter watched the pigeon. "I had a visit this morning from a Miss Metcalfe."

"Rosemary Metcalfe. . . ." Dr. Hill sent another grape in the pigeon's direction. "Works in the library. Nice girl."

"She really came to see you. She's worried about her uncle."

"They've been worried about him for a long time," murmured Dr. Hill.

"She put me in the picture. What sort of person is she?"

The black eyebrows tried to reach white hair. "Interested already?"

"Not in that way. I gathered her intention was to enlist your help in having her uncle sent to an Institution."

"I don't believe that for one minute," observed Dr. Hill.

"She made it very clear."

"Then Garvey's condition must have changed. Which is damned odd. He's been the same for as long as I've known him. Admittedly, the accident didn't help matters, but that only aggravated his condition without changing its nature. He's more a burden to himself than anyone else. Did she give any reasons for wanting him sent away?"

"Only that she felt it was getting her down. She's looking after him at the moment. Did you know her mother was in hospital with a nervous breakdown?"

Dr. Hill was startled. "No, I didn't. Is she in here?"

"I suppose so. And my impression is that it wouldn't take much to push her daughter over the edge as well."

Dr. Hill said: "You might ring the bell. It's by the bed."

Peter dropped to his feet, went into the ward and pressed the bell. When he returned he found the pigeon had usurped his place. He leaned against the side of the window and watched its cautious, sidling progress towards the open bag of grapes.

"You asked me what sort of person Rosemary is," said his uncle. "I brought her into the world, and I'm damned sure I know everything there is to know about her. She's levelheaded and sensible. And her mother is the same—placid and unimaginative into the bargain. So far as I know she's had no trouble with Garvey since he went to live with her after the accident.

"The accident was a tragedy in more ways than one. Rosemary's father was killed, and if Garvey had completed the trip to London the odds are he would have agreed to a course of psychiatric treatment with a good chance of overcoming his phobia. As it was, after his discharge from hospital he refused to see me or any other doctor. Medical men became his enemies. If I hadn't persuaded him to make the trip, and if the psychiatrist hadn't agreed to see him, he wouldn't have been in the train when it crashed. Reasoning distorted by—"

He broke off as the door opened to admit a nurse.

"Was that your bell I heard ringing, Doctor?" she asked him.

"It was." Dr. Hill smiled genially. "But not for my personal needs. Tell me, Nurse, do you have a Mrs. Metcalfe in here as a patient?"

She nodded. "She was admitted a week ago."

"And her trouble?"

The nurse hesitated, eying Peter warily.

"My nephew," explained Dr. Hill. "Also a doctor, and in practice with me. Mrs. Metcalfe is one of his patients."

"I see." She smiled, nodding towards Peter. "One of the fraternity. Mrs. Metcalfe is recovering from a bad nervous breakdown."

"Do you happen to know anything about the circumstances of her admittance?"

"I was on duty when she was brought in, Doctor. It was quite late at night, and a Mr. Milton came with her."

"Milton." Dr. Hill cocked an explanatory eyebrow at Peter. "Another old patient of ours. Retired schoolmaster; nice old boy, even if a bit long-winded. Lives alone out at Betley Hatch. Mrs. Metcalfe's only neighbour." He turned back to the nurse. "And—?"

"Mr. Milton told us he was actually with Mrs. Metcalfe, in her cottage, when she collapsed. He carried her over to his cottage and left her there while he cycled to the nearest phone—a farm, I think. They brought her in by ambulance. And I'm afraid that's all I know, Doctor."

"Thank you, Nurse. You've been very helpful." Dr. Hill grinned engagingly. "Now I'll let you get back to your tea."

Peter hastened to open the door for her. When he returned his uncle, making cooing sounds, was using a grape to tempt the side-stepping pigeon.

"You know Betley Hatch, Peter?" he asked without turning.

"No."

"You go straight through Colford, and a couple of miles past the Establishment there's a fork. Instead of turning left for Southam you carry straight on over the bridge and past Betley Farm. Betley itself is about another two miles farther on, tucked in a sort of dead-end valley, just a handful of cottages with only two in use. Milton lives at 'Betley Cot', the Metcalfes and Garvey at 'Greymill'."

"What have you got in mind?" Peter asked.

The pigeon was pecking at the finger-held grape, but the holder showed no triumph in his taming achievement.

"Milton carried Mrs. Metcalfe over to his cottage," he said slowly. "She's no light weight. Why didn't he leave her where she was?"

"Because Garvey was in the same cottage?" Peter hazarded.

"No. Garvey's about as dangerous as our feathered friend here."

The grape dropped to the ground and the pigeon took flight in a startled flurry of wings.

"I think it would be a good idea if you were to take a trip out to Betley Hatch," said Dr. Hill gravely. "The sooner the better, I feel. This evening would be as good a time as any."

3

His head had started to ache again, and there was a dull pounding behind tightened temples. Edward Garvey sat on the side of his bed, his thin, almost colourless face resting in his hands, trembling fingers pressed hard against parchment flesh, trying to fight the overpowering urge to lie back, to close his eyes and let frightening oblivion have its way with him.

There had to be some reason for these attacks that came on so suddenly, without warning, at any time. Not an after-effect of the accident, although it was only since then they had come. . . . Drugs, then? His food was being tampered with. How They were doing it, he didn't know. Preparing all his own meals, as he had done ever since he first suspected They meant him harm, hadn't been precaution enough. But he was still alive; up until now his cunning had matched Theirs.

Going without food completely hadn't been the answer. And he had been cunning indeed there—pretending to take the plate then, with Rosemary out of the kitchen, scraping it into the swill-can. But still the attacks had come. They were even more cunning than he had feared.

There was no one—no one—he could turn to for help. For a time he had suspected Martha, but she had gone away—he didn't know why or to where—and still the attacks had continued. Now Rosemary, Martha's girl, was here. Perhaps, only perhaps, she could be trusted. There was no reason why she shouldn't be one of Them, but perhaps she could be trusted. He would have to think about that.

Garvey came to his feet with an effort, pushing himself upright with thin-knuckled arthritic hands against the side of the bed, wincing at their pain, going towards the window, limping on the leg that had been broken, that They had caused to be broken as They were also responsible for his twisted fingers and stiffened side.

The lane outside was empty. It was only at certain times of the day that he saw anyone or anything down there. The early-morning milkman and his clattering bottles; the newspaper boy on his bicycle; the scarlet mail van and the man who brought the groceries. Enemies. And Mr. Milton who lived in the cottage a little way down the lane. . . .

Garvey moved hopelessly from the window. There was a roaring in his ears, the pounding of surf on a shingle shore. The need for sleep was too intense to be resisted any longer. Lying on the bed he let leaden eyelids have their way. But sleep, he knew, would not come immediately. It never did. No matter how insistent the tiredness there was always the time of drifting into a terrifying half-world that was neither one place nor another, where part of him still seemed to be here in the bedroom, and the rest of him in another place, a place that he knew had no reality because it was only the prelude to the dream.

Flat on his back, arms straight at his sides, Edward Garvey drifted into the grey mists of limbo, only partly conscious, not aware enough of his surroundings to hear the sharp crack of splintering glass that came from the room beneath, or the startled cry of pain that followed.

In a little while he fell asleep.

This time there was a difference to the waking. Argred the Freeman opened his eyes and was immediately aware of who he was and where he was.

This was one of the blue-lit caverns of the Old People where there was no way of telling the passage of time, so that he could have been lying here for one day or more. By his parched mouth and the hollow of his stomach he had been here for some time. But the period of resting had smoothed away a little of the pain.

He flexed his hands, stiff rather than painful now, using them to push himself first to his knees—flesh on hard rock, for he was wearing the short, untanned-leather tunic of the Freeman which left legs exposed—then to his feet, standing upright, swaying, steadying himself against the curved wall. There was still the dull agony of pain. He would remember the things that had been done to him at the bidding of the Mind-Healers. One day he would repay them.

He was able to walk, slowly, one hand against the wall, his head swimming from lack of food. There was a place he had to find, but first he must find his way back to the entrance again, to the outside world. If Rhoweena had kept her promise there would be food and drink waiting for him.

After the rescue, with others of the Freemen carrying him—for there had been no use in his limbs—with Rhoweena there to see that Old Lorr's orders were obeyed, he had told them to take him to the entrance to the caves.

They had hauled him bodily up the slope of sliding stones, leaving him on the very edge of the miniature plateau, afraid to go any closer to the entrance. Night, it was, not far from dawn, with the plains stretching away to the sprawling mass of the city. And behind, the towering pinnacles, twisted spires that reached into the sky, tipped by the moons, with the Pendant a glowing arc of brilliants.

When the hard-faced Freemen had gone and only Rhoweena remained, he had told her why he had to go into that cleft of blackness. With every man's hand against him—friend and foe alike now—his only chance of survival lay in the hope that the Old People were more than a legend. She had promised to bring food and water. If she had honoured that promise it should be waiting at the entrance now.

The Glowing Fungus lighted the writhings of the tunnel. Only able to move slowly, there was time to think. A few days ago he had been leader of the Freemen. Now they too were against him. They said he had launched the attack against the Palace without sufficient preparation, blaming him for its failure and for the carnage that followed. Even Old Lorr had accused him, only arranging his rescue from the Mind-Healers to prevent the betrayal of names under torture. Never return, they had told him, or you will die.

But he would return—the Old People had to be more than a legend, an old wife's tale. . . . There had to be secret places inside the mountains that were filled with metals wrought into strange shapes, fashioned into invincible, incomprehensible weapons. With their powers he would be able to take revenge on Freeman and Mind-Healers alike. He would be able to make himself master of the world.

A fork in the tunnel, and the air in the one on the right sweeter, fresher. The ghost-blue of the Fungus was fading. White light melted the shadows ahead. Walk unaided now, head up, shoulders straight, even though every step was pain. He was Argred the Freeman.

He came out of the tunnel, into the thin sharp air and the light of a new dawn. A woman crouched at the foot of the slope, wrapped in the folds of a blue cloak. He called her name and she stirred, came awake, drew the cloak from her face, was on her feet, running towards him and into his arms, her flowing black hair against his breast.

She had never expected to see him again, she breathed fearfully, but she had brought food and water. He drank greedily, one arm still about her shoulders, the cool liquid spilling over stubbled chin and running down his chest. And she had brought a sword, hidden in the folds of her robe.

She watched him eat. "There is still pain, Argred?"

"Pain is nothing," he grunted.

"What did you find in there?" looking fearfully at the cave entrance.

"A man finds nothing while he sleeps."

Her eyes became wide. "You have slept all the time?"

"How long?" he asked, tearing bread and cramming it into his mouth.

"This is the third morning!"

He disguised surprise by nodding towards the plains. "What of those who were once my friends?"

"The killing has stopped. The men nurse their wounds and the women mourn. You will go back in there again? You are still going to search for the Workshops?"

25

"When I have finished eating." He tilted the water-skin again.

"Will you need more food, Argred? Shall I come again?"

He wiped meat-greasy hands down his tunic, considering.

"What is left here I will take with me. Used sparingly it will last two days. Another two days I can go without. Four days will be long enough. . . ."

"If the Workshops exist," she sighed. "If they contain the magical weapons of the Old People. If ever there was a race of magicians called the Old People."

"There was," he said roughly. "Else why the stories? Long ago there was fighting. That we know. The farmers' ploughs turn up rusted weapons and bones. The land was divided against itself. Those who were defeated, perhaps only a handful, fled to the mountains here, seeking refuge in the caverns. . . ."

"Or over the mountains," said Rhoweena.

"No." He shook his head angrily. "The mountains are too tall. Man cannot live in snow and ice and empty air. They came into the caverns. And a long time afterwards they emerged again, armed with the new weapons they had forged, strange, fearsome appliances that could kill from a distance, and others—invisible beams that could penetrate a man's skull and twist his mind.

"But they came out into the sunlight too soon, before there was enough of them, so that even with the magical weapons they were beaten back to the caves again. And the men of the Plains celebrated their victory and were happy. But only for a while. Until the effects of the mind-twisting rays began to tell. And then the Mind-Healers came into being, taking all authority on themselves. The presence of the Mind-Healers is proof of the existence of the Old People."

"Perhaps," sighed Rhoweena.

"It is as I have said," he retorted arrogantly, and knelt to pack what was left of the food in the leather bag in which it had come.

"It was Gorold who betrayed you."

"You have already told me that." He came stiffly to his feet.

"I didn't know of his feelings towards me." She looked down at the stones by her feet. "I thought he could be trusted. He knew where you fled for safety after the retreat from the Palace, and betrayed you to the Mind-Healers. With you dead, he thought I would turn to him."

"We will meet face to face again one day." Argred touched the water-skin with his foot. "How fresh is this?"

"It was filled last night. All the food is fresh. I waited here all yesterday, and when you didn't come I left a sign for you that I would return, and went down to get new food. There was a man—" She paused, frowning. "A stranger. He came into the city yesterday, saying that his name was Kolda and that he had come a great distance looking for you."

"Kolda. . . ." Argred tested the name. "No."

"Tall, very young—little more than a youth. Hair the colour of yours. He said it was important he speak with you."

"I know him not."

"He wouldn't say why he had to see you. He wore the leather tunic of the Freemen."

"Where is he now?"

"He is at the house of Marna the Wisewoman."

"Marna. . . ." Argred, stooping to pick up the food-bag, paused. "My feelings warn me that this Kolda is a spy. He must not be able to find me. But he may persuade Marna to look into her magic pool and so discover where I am. You must take some of the Freemen and kill him."

He slung the two bags over his shoulder, turning his face towards the cave entrance to hide the spasm of pain.

"I will return," he said without looking at her, and walked steadily back into the darkness.

Once the white light of the outside had faded into the misty blue glimmer of the Fungus, he slackened his pace. Each step sent a shaft of agony from his injured leg, each breath—and soon they were tortured—increased the pain in his side. The tunnel walls danced about him. The bags weighed heavy, and he changed their position from one shoulder to the other, stumbling as he did so, dropping after a few more steps to his knees, then finding it impossible to rise again.

He would have to rest while he digested the hastily swallowed food, and then sleep. Setting down the bags he eased himself to the hard ground, using them as a pillow, sinking into oblivion the instant his tawny, matted hair touched the cold leather.

Something, perhaps some small sound, brought Edward Garvey awake. The shards of a dream, the same dream as always, melted away. There was a hazy impression of blue glimmering against greyness, and then the memory had gone completely. He sat up, heedful of the stiffness of his hands and the dull ache in his side. His fingers, when they groped in his waistcoat pocket for his watch, moved slowly, almost refusing to do his bidding. He held the watch at arm's length. It was just eight o'clock.

4

For no particular reason, Peter glanced at the dashboard clock as he swung into the main road. It was a few minutes after eight. There was little traffic about this sunny evening, not even in the normally busy square, but he drove slowly, not particularly relishing the trip to Betley Hatch.

An old man had lost his head and lugged a presumably unconscious woman over to his own cottage, and Uncle Andrew was trying to make a mystery of it. There was a great deal of difference between something that doesn't quite meet the eye and a mystery. "When you've seen Rosemary," he'd said, "slip across and make Milton's acquaintance. You'll find him easy to talk to. And if you feel you need an excuse, tell him—oh, tell him I'm hovering 'twixt life and death and the least he could do is come to visit me."

Another aspect of rural practice. . . . Amateur detection with a dash of sociology. If that's what it was.

With the tree-lined square left behind, Peter accelerated, the shops gradually thinning then vanishing, rows of uninteresting, grey-roofed terraced houses taking their place. There was a straggle of larger, prosperous-looking villas, a handful of new, glossy bungalows, and then the open country.

And on the right, the tall, double-wire boundary fence of the Research Establishment. He looked across an expanse of yellowing grass towards the collection of squat, flat-roofed buildings. Engrossed, he caught a flicker of movement out of the side of his eye,

29

turned quickly back to the road and was only able to brake in time to save running down a young man wearing a black leather jacket who had stepped into the road and was flagging him down with impatient, imperious wavings of his arm.

Recognising him, remembering their previous brief encounter outside the hospital, Peter leaned reluctantly across the seat to open the door.

If the recognition was mutual, the other showed no sign of it. His coarse-featured face expressionless, he slung his rucksack, heedless of upholstery, into the back of the car before Peter had time to speak.

Peter said: "Not so fast. I'm not going to Southam. I'm heading for a place called Betley Hatch, well off the main road."

"Don't let it worry you," drawled the youth, and climbed in to sprawl his length along the seat, head resting on the back, knees jammed against the glove compartment.

"Where are you making for?" Peter asked with forced affability as the car moved away.

The young man closed his eyes as if the question wasn't worth the trouble of answering, slipped two brown-stained fingers into the breast pocket of his jacket, produced a crumpled cigarette, flipped it expertly between his lips and demanded: "Match."

Biting back a retort, Peter shrugged and brought out his lighter, having to lean sideways to hold the flame to the wavering tip.

"On a hiking holiday?" he suggested.

"Save your breath, man," replied the other without opening his eyes. "Forget the entertaining bit."

"I beg your pardon," Peter said, and concentrated on the narrowing road. A not particularly pleasant odour emanated from the seat at his side. It had been some little time, he guessed, since his unmannerly passenger had seen soap and water in quantity.

At the fork he turned to the right, the car swaying with the sudden rise and drop of the hump-backed bridge. On the right was a cluster of farm buildings. Sparse pasture gave way to sloping, uncultivated land with the hills rising steeply behind and starting to close in. Five minutes of twisting lane, and a final bend revealed a row of patently untenanted cottages.

A little way beyond, on the opposite side of the lane, was a solitary cottage that was a marvel of renovation. Red tiles had replaced thatch, the walls gleamed white, creeper framed the tiny front door, and the privet hedge had been trimmed with a mathematical precision. An elderly, white-haired man straightened from leaning on the gate, watching with an interested gaze as the car coasted by. Peter braked. The man was obviously Mr. Milton. And the other cottage he could see, a few yards further on, on the other side of the lane, must be Mrs. Metcalfe's.

"The end of the line," he informed his passenger.

The young man roused himself, jerked the door open, dragged his rucksack over the seat and climbed out. With no word of gratitude, no gesture even, he flicked his cigarette into the air, slung the rucksack over his shoulder and slouched away. Peter climbed out to stand and watch him go. A hundred yards further on the lane petered out, becoming a path that ended at a rusty iron gate backed by a slope of wiry grass, broken by the ghost of a footpath that meandered through clumps of gorse and bracken up towards the hills.

"With his face to the hills," quoted a voice at his elbow. "And a stiff climb ahead. That's if he's thinking of making towards Daventry."

"He didn't tell me his destination," Peter replied without turning.

"I rather gathered that from his brusque departure. A taciturn young man."

Peter turned then. "To call him that," he observed dryly, "would be an understatement. He put me in my place by telling me to shut up. More or less." He smiled, offering his hand. "Mr. Milton?"

"Immediate recognition. The penalty of fame. Harvey Granville Milton. And you, of course, will be Dr. Hill. I recognise your uncle's car."

For a man of his obvious years he had a surprisingly firm grip. But it was a grip that matched his short sturdiness, solid brown face and clear, pale blue eyes. The thin white hair that was brushed straight back from his wide forehead must once have been the same colour as his thick black eyebrows.

"I am told," Mr. Milton remarked affably, "that your uncle will shortly be out and about again. Gratifying news."

31

Leaning against the car, Peter produced and offered cigarettes. They were waved politely aside. "Thank you, no. A pipe-smoker."

Peter said: "He is due for discharge next week."

"So I believe. I rely," explained Mr. Milton, "upon my milkman for the local news. He keeps me well informed. Otherwise I would feel almost cut off from civilisation. Existing on a pension that decreases in value each year that passes means that I am unable to afford the luxury of either a car or a telephone."

"Out here," Peter said, looking about him, "one would think a phone would be necessity rather than a luxury."

"True enough, Doctor." The other smiled. "But the expense is still the same."

Peter turned to glance towards the other cottage. He fancied he detected a movement at the curtain of one of the bedroom windows.

"I imagine," he said carefully, "that you would have been thankful for the phone a week ago, when you had the trouble with Mrs. Metcalfe. I hear you had to cycle to the farm."

"I did indeed," agreed the other feelingly, but still smiling.

"After first having carried her to your cottage. It couldn't have been an easy job."

Mr. Milton's smile tended to become strained. "You seem to know all about it, Doctor."

"Not idle curiosity. I'll shortly be taking over my uncle's practice. Which means Mrs. Metcalfe will become one of my patients."

"I see." The other nodded slowly, his face serious. "I had been wondering at your arrival here. I thought I had the answer, but I may be wrong. Your uncle and I are friends of long-standing. There are, as you must be aware, certain complications connected with the Metcalfe *ménage*. . . ."

"Edward Garvey," Peter inserted.

"A long time ago now, your uncle asked me to act as what one might call an outside observer. Unethical perhaps, from a medical point of view, but I think he felt more at ease knowing that if there was any change in Edward's condition, that perhaps his sister would not care to report, he would still be informed of it. Now he is wondering if Edward has had anything to do with Mrs. Metcalfe's breakdown."

"He didn't mention that." Peter studied the tip of his cigarette. "He's puzzled as to why you carried her over to your place instead of making her comfortable where she was."

There was a short silence.

Mr. Milton produced a pipe and pouch from the baggy pocket of his rather shabby tweed jacket and became very engrossed in ramming tobacco into the bowl.

"I suppose," he said without looking up, "that the small crisis caught me unawares. I lost my head. Not a happy confession for an ex-schoolmaster to have to make. How can one explain one's actions in a time of emergency?"

"Perhaps instinct told you it might be dangerous to leave her alone with Garvey?"

Milton looked up at that, shocked into emphatic denial.

"Edward? Dangerous? Good heavens, no!"

"I wouldn't take you to be the type of person likely to lose his head in an emergency."

"I accept the implied compliment." Mr. Milton returned the pouch to his pocket. "Appearances are often deceptive. I'm no longer a young man with a young man's control." He changed the subject. "Will you be dropping in to have a word with Rosemary while you're here?"

Peter dropped his cigarette to the ground and set his heel on it. To try to change the subject back again would smack of impertinence. He, and Uncle Andrew, would have to be satisfied with evasion.

"I may as well have a talk with her," he said.

"Actually," drawled Mr. Milton, "I was about to step over there when you arrived. We usually share a cup of coffee, for which I have a weakness, about this time of an evening. Edward, as you probably know, spends the greater part of his time in his bedroom. Rosemary seems grateful to have someone to talk to, even an old fogey like myself." He set the still unlighted pipe between his teeth. "Would you have any objections if I were to accompany you?"

If there had been, then Peter was given no chance of voicing them, for his arm was taken in a companionable but firm grip, and he found the one-time schoolmaster walking at his side the few steps

33

down the lane. Milton opened the gate of Greymill Cottage with a proprietary flourish, guided Peter up the narrow, lavender-bordered path and rapped a soft tattoo on the white-painted door.

Miss Metcalfe was startled to find two visitors at her door instead of the expected one. Her smile was strained, perhaps with the effort of overcoming dismay at Peter's presence.

"A dual visitation," Milton announced brightly. "Will the coffee stretch that far?"

They followed her along a tiled passage into a small front room. When she had left them, murmuring that the coffee was almost ready, Peter, in the creaking comfort of a chintz-covered basket-chair, looked about him.

During his fortnight in Colford he had seen the inside of many such cottage parlours, finding them all designed on the same pattern. Much care and attention was lavished on them by the proud owners, who regarded them primarily as showplaces, using them only on special occasions. Invariably they contained the same miscellany of treasured possessions; a clutter of garish, dust-harbouring ornaments; rickety tables draped with green baize; upright piano loaded with framed portraits and floral-papered walls decorated with despondent Victorian landscapes.

But Mrs. Metcalfe's parlour was not quite part of the pattern. There was an odd sort of difference that was immediately obvious.

On the mantelpiece over the curved, black-leaded grate were only two ornaments. A china replica of a rearing horse gave the impression of being one of a pair. The glass vase that was its solitary, unbalanced companion could also have been one of a set. The small table in the window was empty, but indentations in its red cloth showed where three ornaments had once stood. Behind, two of the small panes of the window had been broken and patched with strips of brown paper. The piano top was devoid of pictures. The wallpaper, a bedroom pinkness of rosebuds, was faded. Faded so badly that several rectangles of brighter colour showed where the same number of pictures must have hung until fairly recently.

Mr. Milton, comfortable in a second basket-chair, lighted his pipe, balanced the box of matches on one knee and regarded Peter from beneath thoughtful brows.

"A cheerful little room," he observed.

"Yes." Peter eyed the wall behind a black leather sofa. Three pictures had hung there. He wondered why they had been taken down, and why most of the ornaments had been removed. Miss Metcalfe entered with a laden tray while he was mentally phrasing a query that wouldn't have the sound of impertinent curiosity. When she had come to the surgery she had worn a linen frock with short sleeves. She had changed now to a black skirt and a white, long-sleeved blouse.

Setting down the tray on the table in the window, she said, perhaps for Peter's benefit: "Uncle Edward's in his room. He'll probably be down later to make himself a drink."

She busied herself pouring coffee. Reaching to hand Peter his cup, her sleeve pulled back up her arm so that he caught a glimpse of what seemed to be a bandage fastened just above her elbow.

He leaned forward. "What's all this?"

She drew back a little. "I cut myself on some broken glass. It's nothing. . . ."

He laid his cup on the carpet. "All the same, you'd better let me have a look at it."

"It's nothing," she protested again, but reluctantly allowed him to unbutton the sleeve and roll it back. In one place, blood showed through the bandage.

"When did it happen?" he wanted to know, untying the knot.

"Oh"—she shrugged—"not very long ago."

"As luck would have it," inserted Mr. Milton deftly, "I happened to be on the spot at the time."

"I was wondering how she'd managed to put it on herself." The bandage came away. "A nasty cut. . . ." Peter touched it with gentle exploring fingers. "Quite deep. I'd better put an antiseptic dressing on it. Luckily my bag's in the car."

Milton was on his feet and at the door. "I'll get it for you, Doctor."

"On the back seat," Peter called, and turned back to the girl. The arm he was holding was trembling. "What sort of glass was it?" he asked her. "Was it clean?"

She nodded. "I think so. It was a mirror. I was polishing it and it slipped and broke against the side of the table."

"Did you bathe it?"

"Harvey—Mr. Milton—washed it."

He came to his feet. "You'd better sit down while we fix you up."

He stooped to pick up the discarded bandage. There was the thud of the car door being slammed, and he glanced automatically, still stooping, towards the window. He was looking directly at the table and the tray. A china milk-jug rose slowly from the tray, hovered in mid-air for a long, incredible moment, then hurtled across the room, over his head, to smash to smithereens against the opposite wall.

5

"A long time ago," Mr. Milton said conversationally, "more years ago than I care to remember, I worked for a time at a private school in a small Norfolk village. Much the same sort of thing was happening at the local Vicarage. I didn't personally witness any of the manifestations, but one of my colleagues did. He told me afterwards that he found the experience more interesting than alarming. But then, of course, he didn't have to live with it."

Pipe in hand, he stood by the window. Miss Metcalfe, on hands and knees, was collecting, piece by piece, the fragments of the shattered jug. Oddly, Peter found her acceptance of the thing, the way she had set about cleaning up the mess with the resigned acceptance of one performing a familiar household chore, even more strange than the weird cause of the littered floor and spattered wallpaper. Her face was turned away from him, but he guessed from the rigidity of her shoulders that it was only with an effort that she was holding herself in check. He looked at Milton who was still talking, knew why he was using that calm, steady voice, and mentally thanked him for it.

"More things in heaven and earth," the ex-schoolmaster quoted tritely. "And this sort of thing isn't all that uncommon. From time to time one reads of them in the newspapers. More often than not, I feel sure, they receive no general publicity. Perhaps one day we will find the scientific cause of the manifestations at present attributed to poltergeists. It is simply a matter of cause and effect. Until the discovery of electricity, lightning was a supernatural thing.

"If you had seen me pick up that jug and fling it against the wall you would have been puzzled but not alarmed. If you had first watched me attaching a wire to it, then jerking on that wire from a distance, you would still not have seen anything strange. The wire being invisible, the jug would appear to move of its own accord, but knowing how it was done, you wouldn't be alarmed. If we knew what invisible force was responsible for the things that have been happening here—"

Meeting Peter's gaze, he paused, looking slightly abashed and lapsed into silence. Rosemary came to her feet. Peter, at the strain in her face, took her arm and guided her to a chair.

"You'd better sit down, Rosemary. . . ." He used her first name unthinkingly. When he held out his cupped hands she obediently emptied the china debris into them. He went into the hall and found his way to the kitchen. There was no trashcan in sight so he piled the pieces alongside the spotless sink. From a shelf he took down a tumbler, filled it with water and took it back to the parlour. Opening his case he selected a bottle, tipped two tablets into the girl's hand and gave her the glass.

"Sedative," he explained briefly, and stood over her while she swallowed them, looking across at Milton, asking: "Just how long has this sort of thing been going on here?"

"A little over three months. Of late it has been getting worse."

Peter snapped his case shut while his eyes travelled round the room again.

Milton smiled faintly. "As you can see, there is little of a moveable nature that is still left intact."

"A poltergeist. . . ." Peter shook his head. "It's incredible. I've read about them; I suppose I accepted them. But when you see it with your own eyes—"

"A very different story," the other finished for him. "Personally, I feel that the name 'poltergeist' is unfortunate. Literally—mischievous ghost. Mischievous, yes—I'll go along with that, inasmuch as there seems no rhyme nor reason to its activities. But ghost—no. That has a ring of the supernatural. Perhaps, when the causative force is discovered, they will rename it."

Peter looked down at Rosemary. She nodded when he touched her freshly-bandaged arm.

"It was the mirror that hung over the fireplace. It sailed into the window. Glass flew everywhere." She managed a smile. "I'm learning to take it in my stride, Doctor."

"I don't feel very much like a doctor right now," he told her. "My first name is Peter."

"It's odd," Mr. Milton inserted cheerfully, "how adversity tends to break social barriers. The London blitz was a case in point. My friends, the few that remain, address me as Harvey. At least we can thank our poltergeist for breaking the ice. I'm glad, Peter, that you have been able to see something of its activities for yourself."

"I'm not sure that I am." Peter rubbed the side of his nose. "It rather tends to take the ground from under one's feet. But it answers one question that had been puzzling me—the reason for Mrs. Metcalfe's breakdown."

"She endured it longer than I would have thought possible."

"And you say it seems to be getting worse?"

Harvey nodded gravely. "It would appear so."

Peter turned back to the girl. "You can't stay here."

Harvey answered for her. "It's easy enough to say that, but there's Edward to be considered."

"He knows nothing about all this," Rosemary explained. "Things never seem to happen when he's up and about, always when he's upstairs in his room. I've tried to tell him, but he just doesn't listen. When I tried to tell him we ought to leave the cottage, it was the same."

"Which is why you came to see me this morning." He was conscious of relief at the discovery.

"I hoped Dr. Hill would try to talk to Uncle, even persuade him to leave here."

"It wouldn't have done any good," Harvey put in quietly from the window. "Since his accident, the last person Edward would listen to would be a doctor."

"You can't carry on here with things as they are," Peter told Rosemary forcibly. "You know what happened to your mother. . . . You've got to make your uncle listen."

"There is a certain complication," Harvey said. "Some time ago, when all this first started, I discussed Edward's case with Dr. Hill, not mentioning the reason—at Rosemary's request—why we wished him to leave the cottage. Dr. Hill said that in his opinion, any attempt to use force on Edward might provoke a change in his condition. And any change could only be for the worse."

"The last thing I want to do is hurt Uncle Edward," Rosemary said quietly.

"An invidious position," Peter said heavily.

"There is one thing. . . ." Harvey looked doubtfully at the girl. "We have discussed it before, but Rosemary is reluctant."

"Exorcism."

"Not in the religious sense of the word. To my way of thinking—but I am open to argument and correction—the service of exorcism as performed by a clergyman would tend to bring the level down to one of near-superstition. I feel that it should be approached on a more scientific basis. There are those people who possess talents of a kind, which, for want of a better term, I call 'perception'. Mrs. Cookson is such a person."

"She owns a domestic employment agency in Padham," Rosemary supplied for the benefit of Peter's frown. "I know her to speak to from coming in the library."

"Rosemary thinks that the presence of a stranger would upset her uncle," Harvey said. "She feels too that an investigation, perhaps some kind of seance, might prove dangerous." He smiled. "She is more afraid of the cure than the illness. But cure, or the attempt at a cure, there will have to be. It is the only thing." Looking now at Peter, he was no longer smiling. "I am hoping you will add your persuasions to mine."

Peter looked about him with a mixture of small resentment and a great deal of helplessness.

"It's taking me all my time to accept the evidence of my own eyes without trying to find some way of putting an end to it. This is something completely out of my province."

"So we turn to someone whose province it is."

"What sort of person is this Mrs. Cookson?"

"Not the type you are probably imagining. A middle-aged widow, sensible, trustworthy and very efficient. She has to be, to run a business on her own. I first read about her in a local paper some years back. She had tackled, with some success, a problem not unlike this." He paused.

"My opinion is that anything is worth a try. To ask for her help could do no harm, even if it did no good. One calls a plumber to a leaking pipe, or a sanitary inspector to an obnoxious smell on the landing. . . ." Harvey's smile was almost a grin. "And I am given to understand that doctors are not above calling upon the services of a specialist when they come up against something outside their ken."

"It's not quite like that," Peter said, "but I take your point. All the same, I'd much rather you didn't ask my advice."

"There being no provision for such contingencies in the Hippocratic oath?"

"Something like that."

"I have Peter in a spot," Harvey informed Rosemary. "His willing spirit is on my side, but his fleshly qualifications enforce weakness."

She lifted slim shoulders in tired resignation.

"Do what you think best," she said wearily.

Harvey escorted Peter back to the car. It was an hour later, an hour that had passed uneventfully, almost pleasantly, despite the undercurrent of tension. Edward Garvey hadn't put in an appearance, and there had been no sounds at all from his room.

"I hope," Harvey said as they reached the car, "that you don't feel I have bludgeoned Rosemary into accepting something against her wishes. It must look that way, but things can't go on like this, and I feel in my own mind that an investigation of the kind Mrs. Cookson can provide may be the answer. I must apologise for the way I used you as a lever. . . ."

"The means," Peter said dryly, "justifying the ends."

"But you are still not prepared to agree or disagree with me." The other stooped to knock out his pipe against the heel of his shoe. "Having gone through it myself, I have some idea of how you are feeling. You have witnessed something contrary to normality. As you said yourself, it rather tends to remove solid ground from beneath one's feet. Oddly, one can adjust oneself to it to some extent. I understand there are families who have lived with a poltergeist in their midst for quite long periods of time. They must have had ample opportunity for studying its behaviour." Harvey became engrossed in the bowl of his pipe. "I have done a certain amount of studying myself. In fact, I may have been responsible for this evening's demonstration."

Peter stared at him. "You—?"

"On the face of it, the incidents appear to have been haphazard. But I have noticed—without saying anything to Rosemary—that a violent sound is very often followed almost immediately by a manifestation."

"Which is why you slammed the car door more loudly than was necessary?"

"I wondered if you had noticed. Yes. And as you saw, the experiment succeeded. But there my usefulness has to end. Apart from the call I shall make on Mrs. Cookson tomorrow. I should be able to interest her enough in the affair for her to agree to pay us a visit. And, Peter, I would feel much happier if you could be there at the same time. In your professional capacity."

Peter said slowly: "Rosemary isn't my patient, you know."

"Ethics again. Then come as her friend."

"I'm hardly that, yet."

"I think you're weakening," smiled Harvey. "I haven't been a schoolmaster for nothing. Then come out of curiosity. It should be an experience. There is a fascination about things inexplicable."

Peter climbed into the car. The other closed the door behind him; softly, he noticed, careful not to make any loud sound.

"I'll let you know Mrs. Cookson's reaction tomorrow," Harvey promised before stepping back.

It took a few minutes to reverse the car in the narrow confines of the lane. As it moved away, Peter turned to raise his hand, and at the same time look up at the bedroom window. The curtains were still.

Edward Garvey was asleep.

42

And in the tunnels and caverns of the Mountains of the Lost Moon, Argred the Freeman pursued his search for the Workshops of the Old People.

He had been trudging for a lifetime. Time and distance had long ago ceased to have significance. He could remember no time when he hadn't been filled with the overwhelming urge to lie down and drift into unconsciousness.

The injured leg dragged. Each laboured step increased the strength-sapping pain in his side, seemed to add to the weight of the food and water-bags on his shoulder, their thongs biting deeply into his palms.

This was a misty blue world of endless tunnels and caves. A pattern had become familiar through repetition. From low-roofed winding tunnel into high-roofed cavern or grotto. From cavern, back into tunnel again, but with always the choice of several exits. He chose at random, marking each intersection, each new tunnel entrance with the jagged piece of flint he carried. There would come a time when he would have to find his way back.

Some of the caverns were vast cathedrals, ceilings lost in darkness, walls distant beyond vision, but echoing emptily to the slightest sound. There was a nightmare grotto of evil-glistening stalactites and stalagmites, growing so close together it seemed there was no passage between their tortured, twisted shapes.

In one place he came unexpectedly upon a stream of oily black water, coming from darkness to be sucked back into darkness. It flowed so sluggishly, its viscid surface refusing to reflect the blue glow of the Fungus, that he was reluctant even to test it. But now his water-bag was empty and dry, and so he stooped painfully, raising a few drops to his cracked lips, finding it acid-bitter and undrinkable.

And ages later he came upon an archway that seemed too evenly shaped, its contours surely too smooth to be the work of nature. He discovered and traced with trembling fingers the faint chiselmarks of the tools of long-ago craftsmen.

But in that moment of surging triumph, born of the knowledge that here was proof that others had been here before him, and those others must be the Old People, a new weakness came, a cold, bone-melting weakness unlike that previously induced by pain and hunger and weariness.

He staggered through the archway, and was in another tunnel, this one so even, with floor, walls and ceiling so regular that it too could not be natural. And here the Blue Fungus grew more thickly, set in regular, even masses on walls and roof. The entrance and this tunnel had to be the work of the Old People. But surely not carved laboriously by hand, not these miles of smooth walls that stretched away out of sight. Some kind of machine—perhaps a burning beam of light able to melt and mould solid rock.

This new passage-way seemed endless, each smooth bend revealing yet another ahead. But at last there was a narrowing, another archway, and beyond, darkness. He stopped, trying to pierce that gloom ahead, wondering why the Fungus had not been set to grow in this new emptiness.

From the wall at his side he scooped a handful of the Fungus, crushing it so that it pulped between his fingers and ran wetly down his wrist. Holding the glowing mass torch-wise above his head, he stepped through the archway bringing the blue light with him. And so Argred came into the Burial Place of the Old People.

There they were in their hundreds, their thousands, standing upright on either side, arms folded across bony breasts, each in its own niche carved from the rock. Grey faces, hideous in death-calm, stared through shuttered grey eyelids into dusty eternity. And perhaps, everlasting, they had indeed been there for an eternity. Fighting superstitious fear he touched one, finding that the flesh and the cloth in which it was wrapped were one with the walls that surrounded it, the same cold hardness.

They had been a race of giants, the men and women of the Old People. Argred, tall amongst his own kind, barely reached to the folded mummified arms, had to bend his head back to look up into the unholy, impassive faces.

The Place of the Dead was long and narrow with many twists and turns. Holding his Fungus-torch high above his head, he passed between the silent rows, the slow shifting of shadows bringing the ghastly friezes to life, so that he could swear heads were turning to watch his passing. He walked as quickly as the new weakness would allow, forcing his gaze ahead, away from the countless niches and their fearsome occupants.

And then, in this silent world of the dead, where he should only be able to hear the soft pad of his feet and the labour of the breath in his throat, his ears suddenly caught an alien whisper of sound. It brought him to a halt, panic tight in his chest. He forced himself to turn round, for it was from behind that the sound had come. The dying glow of the Fungus reached only a few feet into the darkness now. There was nothing to see, nothing moved, but the sound came again, nearer, an echo of the padding of his own feet.

If he had heard it anywhere else but here, in this awesome place, he would have gone to seek the cause. But now, for the first time in his life, he experienced blind, unreasoning terror. He forced sluggish, nightmare-leaden limbs into staggering movement. For an age he fought weakness and fear. The rows of the dead finally came to an end. Smooth walls narrowed to a door. There was no reason left with which to marvel at a door of dull black metal. It was an obstacle in the way of flight from the still following sound. Dropping the leather bags he tore at bolts that, sliding back, raised a small cloud of dust that clung to his sweat-soaked face. A roaring in his ears drowned the sound of their sliding, drowned too the soft pad of footsteps behind and a voice that called. There was a spreading blackness behind his eyes that had to be fought.

The door swung silently open. There was nothing beyond, nothing but darkness. Not even a floor, it seemed, for when he placed one foot over the threshold it met no resistance, and he only saved himself from falling by reeling back, reaching out to clutch the side of the door. The new weakness could no longer be denied. He swung round, facing the way he had come, seeing in the last few moments before unconsciousness claimed him the shape that came from the shadows, a shape wrapped in some kind of cloak.

He called: "Rhoweena . . ." and slid to the ground, unconscious before he reached it, fingers raking down the cold metal of the door, leaving trails of faintly-glowing blue behind.

And Edward Garvey woke with the echo of a voice still ringing in his ears. He was out of his bedroom, standing on the very top of the

45

staircase, looking down into the hall to where Rosemary, dismayed hand to her mouth, stared back up at him.

She called: "Uncle Edward, are you all right?"; and without replying he turned to blunder back to his room, locking the door behind him.

6

Monday mornings, so Mrs. Charnley had informed him on his first day in Colford, were always busy in the surgery. This, Peter's third Monday morning, was no exception. Four new names had been added to the seven already on the visiting-pad. Instead of pressing the bell he opened the waiting-room door and glanced inside to find the place packed. He replied generally to the chorused greeting and took the first patient back into the surgery with him.

He wondered what the reaction of those rows of placid faces would have been if he casually announced that last night he had seen a milk-jug float through the air and hurl itself against a wall. Startled expressions and gaping mouths would greet the announcement, and the room would probably empty the moment he closed the door, its occupants seeking another medical practitioner, one with a more rational outlook on life.

Mr. Brownlee of the burnt hand was the fourth patient. Peter, who hadn't expected to see him again, at least not with the same complaint, raised interrogatory eyebrows.

Brownlee was still able to supply a grin.

"Gave me fair old gyp in the night, Doc. Nurse 'ad a shufti at it as soon as I got to work, an' she said I'd best come straight to you."

Peter unpeeled the dressing. There was a circle of puffy redness round the injury. He glanced up. "A soldering iron, you said?"

"That's right. . . ." But the patient hesitated.

Peter took new dressings from the wall cabinet. Without turning, he said: "I've treated soldering iron burns before. I know what they look like, how they usually react to treatment. Are you sure that's what this is?"

"That's what it's got to be, Doc," said Brownlee uncomfortably.

"So it's like that." Peter returned with the dressing. "And you expect me to treat a burn that's been caused by something I don't know a damned thing about."

The other looked more bird-like than ever.

"A few wrong words from me, Doc, an' they'd 'ave my guts for garters. You know 'ow it is in places like that." Which was clearly as much as he was prepared to say.

It was midday before surgery was through. Calls occupied another couple of hours. Peter was very late for lunch, but Mrs. Charnley had made provision for that, timing his return with a nice degree of accuracy, bringing plate from oven to table at the precise moment he drew up his chair.

Hospital visiting hours during the week were from three till five, but it was almost four o'clock when he arrived at the small private ward. Dr. Hill, in his favourite chair on the terrace, grinned knowingly.

"Monday morning full house. I know. I'm glad they're keeping you on the go. Any more snags to report?"

Peter hoisted himself to the balustrade. There was no sign of the grape-avid pigeon.

"Snag is an understatement," he said. "I've got something that'll make you sit up and take notice."

"A poltergeist?" demanded Dr. Hill a few minutes later. "You're not serious. . . ." About to laugh, he changed his mind. "No, you mean it."

"I saw the damned thing in action, Rosemary's nursing a bad cut on her arm from a flying mirror and her mother's in hospital with a breakdown. At least we know now why Harvey carried Mrs. Metcalfe over the lane. There was a couple of breakings in rapid succession, her nerve finally broke and he lugged her away to more congenial surroundings."

"I'm damned. . . ." His uncle leaned back. "A poltergeist. Smack

48

on my own doorstep. And you actually saw it in action. I'd have given my right arm to have been there."

Peter grinned at the envy in the tone. "I'll bet you would." Then he stopped smiling. "But it's not funny," and quoted Harvey: "Not when you have to live with it."

There was a short silence.

"No, it's nothing to laugh at," agreed Dr. Hill soberly. "Not when it causes a nervous breakdown. I'm beginning to get the picture. Rosemary must be in one hell of a dilemma. Garvey's stuck in his bedroom, refusing to have anything to do with anybody. Rosemary can't leave him, and in due course her mother will be discharged with nowhere to return to but the same cottage. It would take brute force to make Garvey leave, and God knows what damage that might cause. What an unholy mess. . . . Do you have any bright ideas?"

Peter shook his head. "Stalemate so far as I'm concerned. Milton's taken command of the situation. He's persuaded Rosemary to let him call in a Mrs. Cookson."

"Harvey has his head screwed on. Cookson. . . ." Dr. Hill employed his sideways frown. "Runs an agency of some kind out at Padham?"

"That sounds like the lady. Apparently she's had dealings with this sort of thing before. I promised to be there at the time."

"I wish I could be there with you," declared Dr. Hill wistfully.

There was a message waiting at the surgery.

"Mr. Milton from Betley was here to see you," Mrs. Charnley informed him. "He said to tell you he's giving a party tonight at eight and he'd like for you to come."

"A party?" said Peter, disguising amusement at Harvey's cloak-and-dagger subterfuge with more appropriate pleasurable interest. "That's very civil of him. Thank you, Mrs. Charnley."

"I'd have thought you'd have picked on someone more your own age to get pally with," she commented, adding with more than a hint of suspicion: "I didn't know he went in for parties."

Peter reached Betley Hatch a few minutes before eight o'clock. Harvey, pottering in his garden with one eye on the road, came to the gate as the car drew up. His pale eyes twinkled.

49

"Glad you could make my party, Peter." After dusting loam fastidiously from his fingers he produced his pipe. "Knowing something of your Mrs. Charnley, I thought it best to make the message obscure. I trust I was successful."

"More or less. But she did inform me that you don't have much of a reputation as a giver of parties." Peter climbed from the car. "So Mrs. Cookson's agreed to try her hand at poltergeist-laying."

"I was kept waiting for almost an hour," the other said with feeling. "Apparently she was under the impression I was in search of a position. When I had explained the reason for my visit she told me she could spare an hour, sandwiched between business visits. A busy woman. When I attempted to give her some idea of our problem she cut me off somewhat sharply, saying that she preferred to form her own opinion. She promised to be here at eight, with the proviso she must leave at nine."

The two walked slowly towards Greymill Cottage.

"How does Rosemary seem today?" Peter enquired.

"I think she is relieved at our decision to find a way of putting an end to the nuisance. But it is a relief tempered by a development of sorts. It seems that Edward has taken to sleep-walking, something he's never done before. Shortly after we'd left last night, Rosemary thought she heard a sound from upstairs, so she went into the hall. Edward was standing on the very brink of the staircase, swaying. She called up to him, but he didn't hear her. She was just starting to go up to him when he woke.

"She says he obviously didn't recognise her for a moment; he seemed frightened, and called down to her—a name—'Weena' or 'Tina' it sounded like. But he knows nobody with a name remotely like either. And then he turned and went back to his room to lock himself in. What do you make of it, Peter?"

"Sleep-walking is a common-enough thing. More often than not it's associated with a disturbance of the mind. Which makes Garvey a very likely candidate, his trouble stemming from the subconscious. It might be just as well if Rosemary were to put some kind of barrier across the top of the staircase. I know that somnambulists are supposed to have some form of guardian angel that prevents them doing themselves harm, but I prefer to be on the safe side."

"I have already suggested that to her," Harvey said, leading the way up the path. At the door he paused. "Incidentally, I have taken a lodger unto myself. A friend of yours. One Clive Murchison."

"Murchison? A friend of mine?" Peter shook his head. "Never heard of him."

The other smiled a little. "Most likely he didn't bother about names. It's the taciturn and not over-clean young man to whom you gave a lift yesterday."

"Oh!" Peter's nod gave way to concern. Harvey was an old man living alone in an isolated hamlet where the only other people were a girl and a mentally-sick man. Appearances can be deceptive, but the individual of the leather jacket, greasy shoulder-length hair and arrogant manner bore the stamp of a city underworld where moral codes are sometimes non-existent.

"Is that wise?" he asked anxiously.

"I must confess that at the time I had doubts. But I had very little choice. Apparently, after leaving you he headed towards the hills, his idea being to keep going until darkness, then find some kind of shelter. But he 'came all over dizzy', as he puts it, and had to sit down for a while. He got worse, turned round and came back.

"I happened to be in my front garden when I spotted him heading unsteadily towards Rosemary's cottage. I went to intercept him"—Harvey shrugged—"for obvious reasons. He almost collapsed in my arms. I helped him back to the cottage and made him as comfortable as I could on the settee. We had supper together. He told me his name, that he was twenty-two—I fancied him to be younger than that—and that he'd come from London. He took to the roads when he left school. Since then, jobless, he's just wandered about. A bleak kind of existence. He spent last night on the settee, ate a good breakfast and seemed much better. But when he tried to walk the dizziness came on again. It was genuine enough. He's slept most of the day."

"Would you like me to take a look at him?" Peter asked.

"I suggested last night that he ought to see a doctor." Harvey smiled impishly. "He went up in the air, stating in no uncertain terms that that was the last thing he wanted." He looked first at his watch and then at the lane. "Our Mrs. Cookson is ten minutes late already." He rapped his soft tattoo on the door. "I thought it best not to mention my temporary lodger to Rosemary; she has enough on her mind as it is. If Murchison still isn't fit to travel tomorrow, I shall insist he see a doctor."

The door opened. Rosemary had changed back to the green linen dress, and the bandage on her arm had been replaced by a broad strip of plaster.

"It seemed so much better this morning," she explained, smiling, when Peter inspected it.

A small saloon pulled up behind Peter's car. Grouped in the doorway they watched its driver climb out and come briskly towards them.

Mrs. Cookson, briefcase under her arm, wore an austere tweed suit, thick stockings and low-heeled shoes. Upswept, black-rimmed spectacles were the finishing touch to a business-like appearance. All her movements were purposeful, her way of talking crisp and concise. Harvey's attempt at formal introductions was ruthlessly cut short.

"My apologies, Mr. Milton, for being ten minutes late. Miss Metcalfe; we have met in the library. Dr. Hill; I have met your uncle. . . ." Talking, she carried them with her, herding them into the hall, barely giving Rosemary time to indicate the parlour before flinging the door open and bustling inside, depositing her briefcase on the table and loosening her jacket in the same movement. When Rosemary made to speak she held up her hand.

"Please no. I would prefer to go about this in my own way. There are questions I will have to ask, but first there is a simple explanation I like to make on such occasions as these. I want it clearly understood that I am not a medium. I shall not go into a trance and produce ectoplasm from my bodily orifices." She paused, smiling for the first time to indicate that the announcement had to be taken humorously. "What I intend doing is simple and undramatic. I will make a tour of the house, absorbing atmosphere. Then I will open my mind. There will be no drawing of circles, no holding hands round a table. I would like you all to behave perfectly normally. . . ." She looked about her. "I take it that we here are the entire occupants of the house?"

Rosemary explained with matching brevity about her uncle.

"A pity," declared Mrs. Cookson. "An unpredictable influence. Unfortunate, but unavoidable. Mr. Milton has explained that you are apparently being troubled by a poltergeist. I assume that the manifestations have followed what we have come to accept as the normal pattern—the lifting and sometimes breaking of small objects; foul smells that appear to have no natural origin; rappings on woodwork; the starting of small fires; the introduction of alien substances. . . ."

Rosemary looked helplessly at Harvey.

He said: "As you can see, Mrs. Cookson, this room has been almost denuded of ornaments and pictures. The same applies in some degree to the remaining rooms, with the one exception of Mr. Garvey's bedroom. So far as we know, nothing has happened there. But there have been no foul smells"—he directed a questioning look at Rosemary who shook her head—"no rappings, no fires. I'm not sure what you mean by 'alien substances'."

Mrs. Cookson was frowning surprise at his cancelling of most of the items on her list.

"The appearance of things from some other place than the cottage itself. Usually stones or lumps of earth."

"Nothing like that," he assured her.

"Not the normal pattern then." She set her hands together in the attitude of one about to pray. "A new departure. A challenge." Her prayer-clasped hands pointed at Rosemary. "You have a younger sister, an adolescent?"

Rosemary shook her head. "No."

"But a child has been living here?"

"There hasn't been a child in the cottage for as long as we've lived here. Probably much longer than that. . . . Before we came, an elderly couple lived here on their own."

Mrs. Cookson's palms came apart and plucked eyebrows lifted above the black rims of her glasses.

"Something very different from the usual run. Indeed, so different that I suspect we may not be dealing with a poltergeist at all, but with some other intruding force. How long is it since the manifestations started?"

Harvey took over the receiving end of the interrogation again.

"About three months."

"Who was living here at the time?"

"Miss Metcalfe, her mother and her uncle."

"Her mother. . . . She isn't here now?"

"She was admitted to hospital a little over a week ago."

"Which means Miss Metcalfe and her uncle have lived here alone since then. And the manifestations have continued?"

"If anything," he told her, "they have intensified."

"Then there is one common factor," declared Mrs. Cookson with satisfaction. "Miss Metcalfe's uncle. We are making progress. Now I would like to see round the cottage. No"—when Rosemary made to rise—"on my own." She closed the door behind her. They heard her footsteps in the hall, the sound of the kitchen door being opened.

Harvey looked at Peter. "What do you think?" he asked in a low voice.

"She gives an impression of efficiency," Peter said cautiously.

"Yes. Do we leave her to her own unaided devices?"

For a moment Peter was puzzled. Then he remembered the door-slamming that might have triggered off the milk-jug episode. "Best let her do things her own way," he said, and turned to Rosemary. "This isn't upsetting you?"

Footsteps echoed on the stairs and she looked anxiously at the ceiling.

"I didn't tell her which was Uncle's room. I hope she doesn't disturb him. No"—she smiled at Peter—"it's not as bad as I imagined."

The footsteps came back down the stairs and Mrs. Cookson re-entered the room as briskly as she had left it.

"One bedroom locked," she said to Rosemary. "Your uncle's room, I expect. Will he be asleep?"

"Probably," Rosemary replied.

"A man," Mrs. Cookson announced generally, "tall, young; I get the impression of fair hair. And arrogance, I think. Does that mean anything to us?"

She was looking at Rosemary who took only a few moments to make her decision. "I know of no one like that."

But there was one person to whom that description applied. Peter

54

glanced quickly at Harvey who nodded, agreeing that he too recognised the description of his lodger, then shrugged, raising his hands in a vague negative gesture.

Mrs. Cookson was disappointed.

"The impression is here, in all the rooms. Very clearly. I cannot be mistaken. Will you please all be seated."

Peter lowered himself to one of the basket-chairs, facing Rosemary who already occupied the other. Harvey, arms folded, compromised by leaning against the window sill. Mrs. Cookson, in the centre of the floor, briefly consulted her wristwatch, frowned at its message and closed her eyes. There was silence.

Peter moved uneasily, feeling that the thing was taking on the semblance of some kind of charade. Curious about the method Mrs. Cookson would use in her attempt to lay the poltergeist, he wasn't impressed by her impression-gathering tour of the cottage, nor by her glib description of Clive Murchison. Sensationalism rather than science. . . .

Mrs. Cookson's voice startled him.

"Freeman. . . ." Her eyes were closed. "Does that name mean anything? Arthur. . . . No—something more guttural. . . . But I get 'Freeman' very clearly."

"I don't know anyone of that name," Rosemary said.

"Albert. No. Alfred? Something like that. A foreign name, certainly. . . . Or old Anglo-Saxon?"

Mrs. Cookson fell silent again. Peter glanced under his brows towards the window to see what Harvey was making of all this. And the ex-schoolmaster was leaning forward intently, plucking with thoughtful fingers at his bottom lip, frowning, staring at the floor, as one might do if trying to bring a name to mind.

Mrs. Cookson's voice came suddenly, loudly.

"Who are you?"

Then a silence of expectancy, the air electric with tension.

"We know you are there. Tell us your name."

Her eyes were still closed, but now her head was turned to one side in the attitude of listening.

"Don't be afraid." Her voice had an odd echoing quality. "We only want to help you."

Chill touched the base of Peter's spine. He shivered, turning the movement into a shake of self-annoyance, glancing covertly at Rosemary. Her face white and intense she was staring at Mrs. Cookson, a rabbit hypnotised by a snake. Suddenly angry, Peter was on the point of coming to his feet to put an end to the thing when Mrs. Cookson relaxed, sighed and opened her eyes.

"No. . . ." She shook her head. "Almost—on the very verge—but not quite. And whoever he is, he is so very near. The place is full of his presence, and the impression of fear. We must try again."

She looked at her watch. "But it will have to be some other time. Even at a time like this, business must take precedence. Let me see—shall we say tomorrow evening, a little later; nine o'clock?"

With no time to spare to wait for confirmation, she collected her briefcase, tucked it under her arm, treated them to a bright, professional smile and opened the door. Rosemary had to hurry to be able to attend to the politeness of seeing her out. Her visitor had one final speech to make. She made it while she checked her appearance in the hall-stand mirror, adjusting already aligned spectacles, patting already immaculate hair.

"One thing I can say with certainty, Miss Metcalfe. Your uncle is in some way connected with the things that have been happening here. My impression of the young man is closely allied with my mental picture of your uncle. How that can be, I hope to find out tomorrow. But it is nothing to be worried about. He will merely be the unconscious vehicle, the relay station, as it were. You are quite sure he has been asleep all this time?"

"I'm almost sure," Rosemary told her. "When he's awake I can usually hear him moving about."

Edward Garvey was indeed asleep, had been so for some time, first drifting into his strange half-world of nothingness, then falling asleep at the same moment as Argred the Freeman woke to find himself lying on the ground alongside the metal door that led from the place of the dead into empty blackness.

7

Argred the Freeman opened his eyes and knew in the same moment who he was, where he was and that someone was bending over him. Someone, in the dim blue glow, whose face was shrouded and whose shape was hidden in the thick folds of a cloak.

But not Rhoweena, for here was the sour smell of age, and the hand that clutched the folds of cloth was thin-knuckled and withered. Raising himself with an effort he tore musty wrappings away, revealing parchment brown flesh, sunken eyes and hawk-beaked nose.

He said "Marna," without surprise, for who—apart from Rho-weena, who might have been driven by love for him—would have dared enter the caves than Marna the Wisewoman, the soothsayer, the maker of magic?

Scorning her gesture of help he struggled to his feet, panting even from that small exertion, to stand on legs barely able to support him. The old woman watched impassively, her hood falling back, tangled grey hair straggling to her shoulders.

"Why have you followed me?" he demanded harshly.

Thin lips moved over yellowed, broken teeth.

"Because there are things I know. Because it is ordained. Because there is one who must come to you, through me, and be part of your future."

That was always her way of talking, speech-riddles to mystify. She was a seeker of mysteries, a distiller of evil potions, a listener to the silent voices of the dead, able to read the messages of the future in the still water of her magic pool.

"What are these things you know?" he asked.

Instead of replying she slid a thin ankle from beneath the cloak, touching the leather bags with a vein-ridged foot.

"Food and water," he said, seeing the movement as a question. "Have you eaten and drank from them?"

"Am I a fool, woman?"

Her foot pushed the bags aside. One opened and precious water flowed, a dark pool on the ground.

"Leave them," she ordered when, exclaiming angrily, he stooped. "They are poison."

He stared at her, not understanding.

"The woman Rhoweena put the drug in. She was ordered to do so by her father. If you have touched their contents then you are dying. It is beyond even my power to save you."

"You lie!" he flung at her, but knew it had to be the truth, that Marna, being what she was, would never need falsehood to further her ends. He might have expected Old Lorr to join his enemies, but not that he would take Rhoweena with him.

"It is ordained," said the old woman calmly. "The future was plain in the pool. But a future beyond my understanding. It says that you are to die, yet still live; a future that folds back upon itself and so lacks reason. I searched deeper, learning then of the poison and how the first part of the prophecy will be fulfilled. The second part, that you will still live, I thought to bring about by reaching you before you ate of the poison. But I am too late, and so your future lies in other hands, perhaps in those of the one who waits to come to you."

"And who is this 'one' you babble about?"

"A stranger; a beardless youth. He came to me, seeking where he might find you, Argred, saying that he had come a great distance, driven by a compulsion beyond his understanding. His name is Kolda."

"Rhoweena spoke of him." Argred tossed the name aside. "He is a spy."

"He is no spy," Marna said earnestly. "He spoke under the influence of the truth-drink. He intends you no harm."

"He cannot give me back my life," Argred said.

"There are mysteries," sighed the old woman, "beyond even my understanding."

He turned to stare into the utter blackness beyond the door. "But perhaps not beyond their understanding."

"The Old People," she said.

"They made machines that could take life. Perhaps they also made machines that could restore it."

"There is another mystery I am unable to decipher," said Marna in her cracked voice. "One that you must have seen for yourself unless the poison had already dulled your wits and blinded your eyes. These behind are the dead of the Old People. Reason tells me that, but it doesn't tell me how they came to be as they are. Did you see their faces, Argred the Freeman? Did you see their bodies? There is no age in their faces, and their bodies are whole, without sign of wound or scarring. And yet they died. And you speak of them restoring life. It seems to me they took life from themselves before their spans were run."

"It seems," he mocked, "that there are many things beyond the understanding of Marna who calls herself Wisewoman."

"Spare what little breath you have left," she retorted. "Heed the knowledge I have brought you. Both death and life await you, Argred the Freeman, and Kolda the stranger is part of it."

"Then bring him to me," he commanded, "and let us see what truth lies in your reading of the future."

"He waits at the entrance." She gathered the folds of the cloak about her. "It is a long journey I make for your sake, and without gratitude, it seems."

"Bring him, woman!" he snarled, and turned his back on her, facing the black emptiness ahead.

When the soft padding of her feet had gone, he stretched out the hand that still held the faint glow of the Fungus. There was enough light left to melt some of the darkness at his feet, turning what he had first thought to be an empty abyss into the top of a flight of metal steps.

As his weight came down on that first step so the world was suddenly filled with light; not the blue glimmer of the Fungus, but a blinding, eye-searing brilliance that made him raise one arm to shield his face. And from far away, gradually increasing in volume, came a soft humming sound. After a while, when he judged it safe to expose his eyes again, he lowered his arms and gazed about him in wonderment, knowing that he had found the Workshops of the Old People.

The place stretched away as far as the eye could reach, the distance melting into haziness. The light, white and glaring, came from ribbed apertures in the lofty curved ceiling. It gleamed on the metal of the machines, countless numbers of them, each mounted on a stone pedestal, line upon line of crouching metal monsters, stretching away to infinity.

They seemed lifeless, these strange machines. Covered with a smooth, moulded skin of metal there were no parts that might move. But when he stopped by one, brought to a halt by weariness as well as curiosity, and rested his hand on the cold cowling, his palm tingled with vibration.

And it was in that moment that he had the impression of invisible watching eyes. So vivid was the sensation that, forgetful of the poison-induced weakness, he swung sharply round. But the place was empty of life. The bones of his legs became water, and he clutched for support at smooth metal. There was a strange smell, a sharp, indescribable tang that caught at the back of his throat. Slowly he slid to his knees, leaning, his face against metal, fighting the insidious strength-sapping poison. Blood pounded behind his temples. . . .

Who are you?

He raised one hand to try to wipe away the gathering darkness in front of his eyes. Metal burned cold against his face. Had he heard a voice, or was imagination turning pulsebeat into words?

We know you are there. Tell us your name.

Not imagination. . . . He had heard a voice, but not with his ears. The words had been spoken inside his head. Crouching, one hand still resting on the machine, he peered about him through darkening eyes while superstitious fear flooded his body.

Don't be afraid. . . . Clearer now, more distinct.

We only want to help you.

60

The voices of the dead? he wondered.

The strength had left his hand, the fingers opening, relaxing. The darkness had all but blotted out the light. There were other voices now, talking together, babbling senselessly, drowning his thoughts in a silent cacophony of sound. He slumped sideways, his face coming to rest against the stone plinth. Argred the Freeman closed his eyes and was sucked into the whirlpool of unconsciousness.

And the sound of distant voices brought Edward Garvey awake and sitting up in bed, staring about him while the memory fragments of a dream mingled with the reality-world about him. The dream faded, but the voices he had thought to be part of it were still there, coming from the lane outside. Swinging his legs stiffly to the floor he limped to the window, moving the curtain a fraction while he peered out. There were two cars in the lane; one he recognised as belonging to Dr. Hill. A woman, a stranger to him, was walking briskly towards them. Three people stood by the gate, watching her. Rosemary he recognised, and Milton, but not the young man with the long solid face, firm features and wealth of dark hair.

Mrs. Cookson reversed her car with the smooth precision one might have expected; a faultless manoeuvre, the perfection of which aroused feelings of envy in Peter's breast. She drove away without a backward glance.

"So there we are," observed Harvey generally, breaking the somewhat awkward silence left in her wake.

"I was going to ask her to have coffee," Rosemary said unhappily. "She didn't even give me the chance. . . . I can't help feeling it was all a waste of time. She didn't even try to find what is making the things happen. All she could say was that Uncle Edward was responsible and for me not to worry. Do you think I ought to let her come again?"

"She seemed to take acceptance for granted." Harvey produced his pipe with a grunt of relief. "But then she is possessed of an almost domineering personality. She was right, of course, in saying Edward was the common factor. That's a simple matter of logical deduction. But I don't think I should attach any significance to that."

"She said he was a relay station, Harvey. What did she mean?"

"I think," he told her lightly, "that we ought to forget Mrs. Cookson and her theories for the time being. Your suggestion of coffee was an excellent one. . . ."

Rosemary fell in with his change of mood. She smiled affectionately at him. "I think you would drink coffee till it came out of your ears."

He shuddered delicately. "You conjure up a terrifying picture. For upwards of forty years I suffered the muddy brown liquid graced by the title 'tea' which was supplied in countless teachers' commonrooms. I have a great leeway to make up in my coffee-drinking."

Filling his pipe, he watched the girl return to the cottage. When she had disappeared he turned to Peter, inviting: "Any comments?"

Peter shrugged. "A neutral observer. I reserve judgment."

"Tall and with fair hair," Harvey mused, replacing his pouch. "Young and arrogant. Eh?"

"Perhaps," Peter suggested dryly, "she spotted your lodger standing in the window."

"I don't think she did. He was fast asleep when I left him." Harvey moulded the tobacco in the bowl with more than necessary care while he went off at a tangent.

"Face, name, background. In any order you like. One leads to the others. That's if you have the knack. Pelmanism; you know the sort of thing. A knack it would pay a doctor, say, to learn. Help inspire confidence in his patients. Face leads to name and history. Eh? All there without having to look up the files. . . ."

Peter, wondering where all this was leading to, listened and waited.

"Pays the good schoolmaster to learn the same knack. Respect of his class for one thing. Another—an anonymous pupil is an overlooked one and therefore a bad scholar. I've had over forty years in which to practice. Boys—all shapes and sizes—thousands, tens of thousands of them. . . . Must be. You know what I'm trying to say?"

Peter smiled. "That you never forget a face."

"Or the name and the background to go with it. Never slipped up once to my knowledge." Harvey folded his arms and rested them on top of the gate, continuing with the short jerky sentences so unlike his normal pedantic manner of speech.

" 'Freeman'; the name she came up with. Common enough. No reaction. Then the other—'Aldred'—or something like it. Put the two together and something clicks. But still not enough. Add the description—Murchison's description—and that fits too. And the name Rosemary said her uncle used—'Weena'. Another little piece. They all fit together. Damn. . . ." He shook his head, frowning. "It'll come back. I'll remember. A long time ago. . . ."

The rich fragrance of coffee that came drifting from the open door behind wasn't sufficient to bring the ex-schoolmaster from out of his reverie. One thing was leading to another. There was a gradual return to his more usual way of speaking.

"It's all here. . . ." The pipe-stem tapped his forehead. "Tucked neatly away. The subconscious. That part of the brain we have no control over. Eh? A kind of complex filing-cabinet. Everything that happens to us, everything we see or hear or read, all filed away. Just waiting for the right key to open it up. But a filing system we can't consciously find our way to. And when we dream. . . ." He paused. "I'm not speaking out of turn?"

"Not where I'm concerned," Peter said. "I've no pretensions to being a psychiatrist. I've dabbled, perhaps rather more than a layman. Enough to go along with your filing-cabinet notion."

"I believe," Harvey said, "that at one time psychiatrists tried to read meanings into dreams. I understand they are in the process of revising that theory. Now, they tell us, we dream from the moment we fall asleep till the moment we wake. Sometimes we can recall the dreams, usually we can't. Dreaming is a kind of haphazard dipping into the subconscious, the type of material we dig out being dependant upon our mood at the time. Or an indigestible late meal. A deranged mind. . . . Eh? Edward. I suppose he dreams. A safety valve. Or a way of escape from the world he's made for himself. Would you subscribe to that theory, psychiatry-dabbling Doctor?"

"Coffee's ready!" Rosemary called.

"Saved by the bell," observed Harvey, returning his still unlighted pipe to his pocket. "Spared the trouble of finding a sensible reply to an unanswerable question. I seem to have been talking for a considerable length of time. But the circumstances are extenuating. I am an old man who lives alone with few people to talk to and fewer still to listen, when I ramble."

They walked up the path.

"Freeman," Harvey fretted suddenly in the hall. "Aldred Freeman. With something—another name—between. And Weena. . . . It'll come."

"Perhaps," Peter suggested dryly, "you once had a dream."

"*Touché*," Harvey said. "I asked for that."

"You asked for what?" Rosemary wanted to know as they entered the kitchen.

"Our young medical friend was putting me in my place," he told her. "But in the nicest possible way. I have the feeling he may be bored with our troubles."

"Far from it," Peter hastened to correct.

The other smiled quiet satisfaction. "Then I take it that you will want to be present again when Mrs. Cookson resumes her activities?"

Privately, Peter felt that so far as he was concerned the thing had gone far enough. Mrs. Cookson might be genuine, he thought that she was—even though poltergeist-laying seemed to have turned to ghost-raising—but that didn't alter the fact that for a medical man, and a newcomer, to be associated with such an affair was very far from clever. If word got around, the practice might suffer.

Rosemary, bringing coffee-pot from stove to table, had stopped and was watching his hesitation with patent concern. A fold of hair had fallen over one side of her face and watching, she pushed it away with her free hand, looking in that moment, he thought, like a small child that had lost its way in a crowded store and was plucking up the courage to ask for help.

Harvey said quietly: "Now we've started, we can't leave it up in the air. We've got to give the woman a chance. Even if it's only a million to one chance, it's worth a try. Especially if we consider the only other alternative." He added: "And if we do go on I think you ought to be here."

Peter nodded slowly, more aware than ever of the strain under which the girl had been living. And with no personal knowledge of Garvey's mental condition he had to accept his uncle's assessment of what his forcible removal from the cottage might mean. Rosemary also knew the gravity of the risk involved. Any decision should be hers.

"I'll do whatever you think best," she said in reply to his look.

Harvey took the thing to be settled. "So that's that." And completely at home in the tiny kitchen, he sorted out a tin of biscuits from the cupboard and brought it to the table.

Peter looked at the girl. "I don't suppose your uncle will be joining us, Rosemary?"

She shook her head. "He never comes down when anyone's here. Most probably he's sleeping."

Edward Garvey wasn't asleep. His body ached and he was tired—tired to the point of exhaustion, but for once sleep refused to come. But then Argred the Freeman was still lying unconscious on the floor of the Workshops of the Old People.

8

The first patient of Tuesday morning's surgery was Mr. Brownlee. "Like a bad penny, Doc." His grin seemed as permanent as it was infectious. "The old 'and kept me awake most of the night. I didn't feel like goin' to work this morning."

Peter removed the dressing. The inflammation had increased and there had been a considerable amount of serum seepage. Sitting back in his chair he eyed the patient sternly.

"We've agreed it wasn't done with a soldering iron. All right. You've got a nasty infection here. I can't go on treating you in the dark. Security's all very well, but I have to know what really caused the burn."

Brownlee's grin weakened. "You know I can't tell you that, Doc."

Peter reached for the phone. "Then I must find someone who can."

The grin faded completely. Brownlee's face changed completely under its new look of apprehension.

"They don't know about it out there, not even the nurse. I'd be kicked out if they knew. Like I said, we're supposed to stay in our own departments; we're not allowed to wander. . . ."

"And you did?"

"I've got a mate, a bit higher up than me, wot works in another building. We 'ave the odd pint together an' he tries to be cagey about 'is work. You know the sort of thing—lookin' down 'is nose. Well. I 'ad a message to take, an' it was an excuse, so I sort of took the long way round which took me through the place where he works."

Peter nodded at the swollen hand. "And that was the result?"

Brownlee nodded shamefacedly. "I should've known better than go pokin' about. I found 'is place but he weren't there. So I 'ad a sort round among the stuff on his bench, an' that's when I caught it. Don't ask me what it was; I didn't stop to find out, even if I could've made sense of it. I just got the 'ell out of it before I was spotted. An' that's all I can tell you, Doc. Gospel."

"You should have told me that in the first place," Peter said. "Not that it's much help. Off with your jacket and roll up your sleeve. Right arm." He went over to the cabinet. Mr. Brownlee's apprehension deepened perceptibly.

"So it's like that. . . ." He winced as the sleeve brushed his hand. "Back in the bleedin' army again. . . ."

Peter had fallen into the habit of visiting his uncle every other day, but because he knew he would be waiting to hear the outcome of the previous evening's visit to Betley he made a point of driving to the hospital as soon as lunch was over. Dr. Hill was in his usual chair on the terrace with the pigeon pecking its way along a line of broken biscuits spread invitingly on the top of the balustrade. Not to disturb it, Peter made his report from the open french window.

"I get the impression," said Dr. Hill at the end, "that you think Mrs. Cookson is something of a charlatan. But don't forget she has a very healthy little business that takes up most of her time. There's no need for her to pretend to be something she isn't. Any help she tries to give must be at the expense of her real work."

"It was the way she set about it, I suppose," Peter said. "A smacking of side-street seances."

"I know what you mean." Producing a fresh supply of biscuit from his dressing-gown pocket, Dr. Hill extended the pigeon-enticing trail. "Something they didn't prepare you for at medical school."

"She's going out there again tonight," Peter said, watching the busy pigeon. "I said I'd be there."

"Did you, now. . . . Mrs. Cookson's activities can't be the bait. Rosemary, then? The country air."

Peter laughed. "I might have expected match-making to be one of the side-lines of a rural practice. No, I have old Milton to thank. He cornered me very neatly."

"He's an expert. Freeman. . . ." His uncle curled a pensive finger in the pigeon's direction. "What was the other name again?"

"Weena? Oh—Aldred, or something like that."

"There was a Freeman who lived out on the Banbury road, but his name was Walter. The only other one I know in this part of the world—"

Peter was startled. "Surely you're not taking it seriously?"

"When you've been in practice as long as I have you'll learn to take everything seriously. It doesn't pay to be incredulous. What does Harvey have to say about all this?"

"He seems to be taking it seriously. In a way, I think he's almost enjoying himself. He thinks the names mean something to him, that he's come across them somewhere before."

"For an old man," said Dr. Hill, "he has an excellent memory. One of the best I've met. But then he's made a point of cultivating it."

"So I gathered," Peter replied wryly. "He treated me to an exhaustive lecture on the subject. With a few comments about the workings of the subconscious mind thrown in for good measure."

"That's Harvey." The other smiled. "A great conversationalist. A pity for his sake that his pocket forced him to bury himself out in the wilds." He paused, turning an eyebrow in Peter's direction. "If he says he's met those names before, then he has. I've never known him make a mistake. So they're real. Which means Mrs. Cookson didn't invent them for the occasion. Which is all very odd, and makes a change from measles and chicken-pox. It would happen while I'm stuck in here."

Peter drove back to Colford through the warm afternoon sunshine. There were only four calls to make, all of them local, before evening surgery at five-thirty. After tea the sky became overcast and a cool breeze sprang up. It was a little after quarter to nine when he drew up outside Betley Cot. As he climbed from the car, Harvey emerged from his front door, still wearing the same baggy tweed suit, but now with a white scarf tucked neatly into the open neck of his checked shirt.

"A change in the weather," he greeted Peter, opening the gate. "Cooler. We old ones feel it. I'm pleased to see you, Peter. I must admit I had doubts as to whether you would come."

"The interest of my unofficial patient at heart," Peter rejoined. "How has she been today?"

The other gave the matter a certain amount of consideration.

"Better, I would say," he decided finally. "More cheerful in herself. I haven't seen Edward; he hasn't stirred from his room all day, apart from a brief visit to the kitchen first thing this morning to get himself something to eat." He smiled sunnily. "And that, Doctor, is my official report."

"And your lodger?"

"He slipped my mind. Yes, he seems better too. He informed me over lunch that he will be hitting the dust—I think that was the expression—tomorrow morning."

Harvey closed the gate behind him and then leaned against it, settling himself for another lecture.

"I spent most of the afternoon in the reading room at the public library. It is surprising how many books deal seriously with the matter of poltergeists. And there are quite a large number of people who appear to possess similar talents to those of Mrs. Cookson.

"Much the same pattern seems to apply to all poltergeistic manifestations. The pattern that Mrs. Cookson described, but which does not appear to apply in this instance. Almost always a female adolescent is involved, her presence appearing to be the link between some unknown force and its outward manifestations. One theory is that the subconscious is the causative factor. There was an analogy I found interesting. The subconscious mind of the adolescent was likened to an invisible body threshing aimlessly beneath an invisible covering, the movements of the limbs being responsible for the inexplicable happenings.

"During the difficult period of adolescence the mind is in a state of tension. One could say that it is deranged. We know the condition of Edward's mind, and we know that a noise can trigger off a manifestation. There is an obvious connection. Mrs. Cookson is probably right when she says Edward is responsible for the disturbances."

"It's a theory, certainly," Peter replied with marked lack of enthusiasm.

Harvey refused to be dismayed by the tone. "It's a theory that fits all the circumstances."

"I was given to understand that Mr. Garvey has suffered most of his life from some form of persecution mania. So why have the things only been happening within the past few weeks?"

There was an answer ready. The ex-schoolmaster delivered it with quiet triumph. "His condition deteriorated after the accident. It was about three months ago that it reached the pitch where he took to spending all his time locked in his room. And that coincides with the start of the trouble."

Peter let it rest at that. He changed the subject. "Have you been able to remember where you heard the names before?"

Harvey shook his head. "Not yet. It's very puzzling. Several times it's been there, on the tip of my tongue, but each time—" He turned to glance back at his cottage. "Murchison. . . . It's odd. Something he said this morning. . . . He mentioned that he usually keeps to the towns and that this was his first time in the country as such. I asked him why he'd wandered this way. He said he didn't know, that he just felt like a change. But he didn't seem too sure of himself. And there was something about it—about his uncertainty of why he'd come here—that reminded me of something that had happened a long time ago. Association of events, perhaps. But in some way tied up with the names."

Peter, with no suitable comment to offer, welcomed the arrival of a car. Having climbed out with only a discreet display of leg, Mrs. Cookson turned to collect the briefcase that was part of her business attire. On her brisk way towards them she consulted her watch.

"Good evening, Mr. Milton; Dr. Hill." A brittle smile and no slowing of her pace. She swept by, leaving them to follow.

Rosemary had the cottage door open. Her smile, a general welcome, rested the longest on Peter. She displayed her arm with its strip of plaster. "It's healing nicely." And there was no time for anything more, for Mrs. Cookson, with the briefest of greetings, was in the hall and already opening the parlour door.

"Has anything more happened since yesterday, Miss Metcalfe?" she enquired from her centre-of-the-floor position.

"No," Rosemary told her, and stepped aside to allow Harvey and Peter to enter the room.

"The presence is still here," declared Mrs. Cookson. "Stronger than before. I was aware of it even before entering the cottage."

She paused, palms together, head on one side, brows drawn together in a faint frown of puzzlement. "But there is a difference. The sense of fear has gone. . . . But there is something else in its place." Her preoccupied gaze rested on Harvey's face. "Resignation?" she asked it. Her gaze moved on. "A negative emotion, always the most difficult to define." Now she was looking at Rosemary. "Your uncle will be in his room?"

Rosemary swallowed nervously and nodded. "He's been there all day."

Mrs. Cookson threw her head back, took a deep breath and closed her eyes. Like the priestess of some obscure sect, Peter thought; surrounded by her acolytes, preparing to launch into the mysteries of some equally obscure ceremony. But still he was aware, uncomfortably so, of the change in the atmosphere of the room.

"I will try again," said Mrs. Cookson.

In the bedroom above, Edward Garvey lay on his bed. He had been asleep for some time, almost two hours. And for the same length of time Argred the Freeman had been awake—conscious but unable to move—lying where he had fallen on the stone floor of the Resting-Place of the Machines.

That was the name that had been put into his mind by the silent voices. That was their name for this place. Once, long ago, they had told him, this had been their Workshop. But now—

Listen, the voices said when he awoke from the sleep he had thought to be the forerunner of death; *open your mind to us. Don't try to talk. Don't be afraid. Listen.* . . .

He had listened. He was a body lying on the floor, with a mind that was no longer his own. No pain, now; no fear. He heard words with his thoughts and saw pictures on the mists of his mind. He listened and saw the story of the Old People.

The legend was true. A great battle had been fought and the few of the defeated people that remained had retreated back to the caves from where they had come. *Only a few of us,* sighed the voices.

And in that long tunnel of the dead, the bodies set upright in the silent niches, the bodies he had thought countless, could be numbered after all.

Less than two hundred, sighed the voices.

They had come back to the mountain to forge new, more powerful weapons, ready for the next time.

But there was to be no next time, yearned the voices sadly.

Something had happened. Something that, even with their limitless wisdom, they hadn't foreseen.

For centuries they had lived in caves lighted by the Glowing Fungus. For three short days, while the battle had lasted, they had been exposed to a new kind of light, that which came from the sun.

The blue glow of the Fungus, they told him, *holds some strange force that we were not aware of. Through the centuries it had been absorbed by our bodies. Exposure to sunlight set the force working within us. . . .*

They had started to change. Their faces had altered; their bodies. . . .

And even greater evils. An end to the bearing of children. As the old ones died—and now they died in their prime—there were no young to take their place. The race seemed doomed. They had turned their energies from the making of weapons to that of self-preservation. They had found an answer. They had built metal bodies for themselves.

The smooth cowled machines on their stone pedestals were the new bodies of the Old People. They had learned the secret of transferring the life-force. They had exchanged corrupted flesh for incorruptible metal. They were linked into a single communal mind, thought and meditation their only ways of passing the lonely centuries.

First, they had destroyed their weapons. But the tools in their making were indestructible, and so they had been taken out of the caves, into the plains, and hidden there during the hours of darkness.

Out in the open? marvelled Argred.

There was a reason for that. There was always the danger that one day men of the outside might find the courage to enter the caves and discover what they concealed. If the tools were to be found nearby, then their uses might be guessed. And they were the only implements capable of destroying the metal bodies. But hidden out in the plains, one piece here, another there, if found, it would be thought they were parts of weapons left over from the long-ago battles.

A man of the outside has found that courage, Argred said proudly inside his mind. He has found some of your secrets. You tell him the others yourself. . . .

We have read your thoughts, the voices told him. *We know why you came. Your enemies are our enemies. You came not to destroy but to seek help. We will give you that help.*

It is too late, Argred thought. I am dying.

Only your body is dying, they whispered.

They knew of the venom coursing through his blood. They knew of Marna the Wisewoman. . . .

We have probed her mind. She will keep our secret.

And they knew of the stranger, Kolda.

He has a young body, breathed the voices softly. *Strong and healthy. . . . What we have done for ourselves we can also do for you.*

Throw the worn-out cloak away, thought Argred without any feeling. Put on the new one.

Your dying body exchanged for a live one, the voices said. *Into your new mind, all our wisdom. We will tell you where the tools are hidden, teach you how to use them to make the weapons. Your enemies will be at your mercy.*

And then they were suddenly silent; watching, it seemed, waiting. . . . Could a thing of metal have eyes?

Argred opened his eyes. From where he lay he could see the flight of grilled steps that led down from the metal door. Marna, a ghost-like grey shape, was coming down the stairs, looking about her in wonderment. And behind her, standing proudly in the doorway, no sign of fear on his arrogant face, was a youth who wore a black leather tunic, and whose hair was a tawny-gold mane that reached to his shoulders.

Kolda the Stranger came down the steps in the wake of Marna the Wisewoman.

One voice spoke alone, softly, urgently, inside Argred's mind.

Tell the youth to stand close at your side.

"A young man wearing some kind of black leather coat," said Mrs. Cookson slowly, without opening her eyes. "Tall, golden-haired. . . . The impression is very clear."

Murchison's description again, now with the added refinement of the clothes he had been wearing. Peter looked at Harvey, but the old man's attention was too deeply drawn elsewhere.

The palms of Mrs. Cookson's hands made hollows of her cheeks.

"The name Freeman is still here. There are many voices, but I cannot hear the words. The young man, I think, is lying on the ground. On something cold and hard. . . . Rock, I think. There is the impression of some place deep underground. A cave?"

She lowered her hands; her eyes were still tightly closed.

"Certainly, some vast, underground place. Deep underground, for there is the sensation of great weight pressing down. But what possible connection can there be between this cottage and a subterranean cavern?"

Peter looked across at Harvey again. And again the one-time schoolmaster missed the look. For he had pushed himself up from his half-seat on the window ledge and was staring at the opposite wall, lips moving soundlessly, his face a mask of startled incredulity.

"Make yourself known to us," Mrs. Cookson said loudly and clearly. "Don't be afraid. . . ."

Make yourself known to us.

The voice was in Argred's mind, but he knew the message was intended for Kolda.

Don't be afraid, the voices added.

74

Standing at Argred's side, Kolda swivelled on the balls of his feet, looking about him, demanding: "Who spoke?"

"No one spoke," Marna said wearily. She had sunk to the ground at the foot of the stairs and was crouching there, bundled in the dusty folds of her cloak, only her carven face exposed.

"I heard a voice," Kolda said, one hand on the hilt of the short sword at his side.

"You heard nothing," sighed the old woman. "There are but we two and a dying man."

Sleep, murmured the voices with a new tone. *You are tired. Sleep. . . .*

"It is there again." Kolda swung round, sword out. "Who spoke?" He staggered, regained his balance, swayed, fell to his knees. The sword clattered to the ground.

Sleep . . . droned the voices softly.

He was lying on the ground at Argred's side.

Sleep . . . hummed the voices, barely audible.

Kolda slept.

Argred, said the voices, *everything is ready. . . .*

Mrs. Cookson shuddered, drew a deep breath, let her arms fall back to her sides and opened her eyes.

"Something happened," she said. "I felt the change. Something. . . ." She gazed about her, frowning, her eyes searching the room. She found the answer. "The presence has gone. The room is empty."

End of charade, Peter thought. Poltergeist-laying completed. And now what?

"You mean there will be no more trouble?" he asked.

"There will be no more," she said simply.

The positive declaration startled him. He had had no faith in her activities. Now it seemed he might have misjudged her. It was one thing to suggest the manifestations might cease; quite another to state so positively that they would. Mrs. Cookson must feel very sure of herself.

She furthered that impression when Rosemary leaned forward, asking hopefully: "Are you sure?"

75

Her voice was calmly confident. "I'm quite sure, Miss Metcalfe. You will have no more trouble."

She consulted her watch, holding her wrist to the fading light of the window. Harvey had her briefcase ready.

"Thank you, Mr. Milton." Her smile now seemed a more genuine thing than those offered earlier in her professional capacity. "And I must thank you also for inviting me here. It has been a most interesting experience."

Rosemary was on her feet, but her anxious attempts first at gratitude, then to play her role as hostess were waved politely but firmly aside.

"I may not have been directly responsible for the removal of the presence, Miss Metcalfe. That is something we will probably never know. I would like to stay, but I have another appointment."

With the two men left alone in the room, Harvey turned to look out of the window.

"An interesting experience indeed," he told the twilight quietly.

"Yes," Peter said.

"Oddly enough I also had the feeling that something had happened. An easing of tension. The sensation of something going away. Hard to explain. . . . The flatness of a sudden anticlimax. Or just imagination?"

The question hung unanswered in the room. The silence was broken by the sound of the front door being closed.

"Coffee," Rosemary announced with a new brightness from the doorway, "will be ready in a few minutes. A pity she couldn't stay. Do you really think it's all over?"

She was looking at Peter, but Harvey turned slowly to face her.

"I don't know," he told her slowly, not answering her smile, which was unusual for him. "I don't know."

"Time will tell," Harvey observed some time later as they stood at the gate. A three-quarter moon sailed across a ragged tear in the clouds sending patches of light drifting across the hills, shadowing the hollows. The cool breeze lifted the strand of hair that had fallen across Rosemary's forehead, and she reached up to brush it aside.

"More things in heaven and earth," Peter said, matching platitude with platitude.

Harvey's teeth gleamed in a fractional smile. "*Touché* again." He yawned hugely, involuntarily, not a hint although Rosemary accepted it as such, laying her hand affectionately on his arm, saying: "It's getting late, Harvey."

"It is indeed." He added for Peter's benefit: "I usually turn in at ten. Early, but one of the penalties of age." He opened the gate. "Good night, Rosemary. Sleep well."

The two men walked to the waiting car.

Harvey was strangely silent.

"So that's that," Peter said lamely, one hand on the car door.

"Yes." Harvey stood there, one hand fumbling absently at the lapel of his coat, his face turned towards the shadowy hills. His reply, lacking finality, hung in the air. After a while, when it showed no sign of coming down, Peter opened the door.

"All of forty years," said the other suddenly, inconsequently. "It must be that. A long time. Memory, even the best, fades. But it was there all the time. Just needing a nudge. . . . Mention of caves. That was part of the connection I was trying to remember before. And the compulsion. . . . Not really compulsion, perhaps." He shook his head. "There was Murchison coming here, for no reason that he could say, and trying to make for the shelter of a cave in the hills. That was the connection."

Peter let him talk.

"It's coming back gradually. I need time to think. The names—I have those. Not 'Aldred'; 'Argred'. Argred the Freeman. And not 'Weena'. 'Rhoweena' it should be. Rhoweena, daughter of—what was his name? Lorr. Old Lorr."

Peter stared at him. "What on earth?"

Harvey turned to look at him then, smiling faintly. "Not on earth, Peter. On a planet called Andrida. How did it go? 'A faraway planet, a million light years away, on the dark, lonely fringes of the Galaxy'. All very romantic. And the caves were the home of the Old People, in the Mountains of the Lost Moon."

"I don't understand," Peter said.

"No more do I. At least, I have a glimmering, but I need time to

77

think. It's incredible, but it makes sense of a sort. There are coincidences, parallels. . . . If what I'm thinking. No—" he broke off, shaking his head. "I must try to sort it out first."

He looked towards Rosemary's cottage.

"It's all to do with Edward. Something very strange has been going on in there. And I'm not so much thinking about the poltergeist. That's only part of it. Something did happen in there tonight, you know. But just what it was—"

Harvey spread his hands, lifted his shoulders in a hopeless gesture.

"I think I know what it might have been," said he. "But if I were to tell you, you'd say I was out of my mind."

To Rosemary, in the kitchen, putting the supper things away, the place felt different. There was a feeling of emptiness, the feeling that something had been taken away. Her father had been a large man, given to much talking and great gusts of laughter, his robust presence filling any room he entered. And leaving, there was emptiness in his wake. This sort of emptiness now. As if some strong personality had just left.

Switching off the light she went into the passage and along to the hall, there to turn on the stair light and glance automatically at the grandfather clock. Equally absently she tested the soil of the potted fern on the hallstand to see if it was moist enough. A small sound made her turn.

Her uncle stood at the top of the stairs, his pale hair haloed by the light, his thin, pallid face expressionless. Jacketless, his flannel shirt was tucked roughly into the leather belt of his trousers. Arms straight at his sides he came step by deliberate step down the stairs, pausing at the foot to smile at her, to say: "Rosemary"—mouthing the syllables as if he found them difficult—"I am hungry. I would like something to eat. Will you get me some food?"

Without waiting for a reply he resumed his clockwork walk along the passage, going into the darkness of the kitchen without bothering to switch on the light.

The girl stared incredulously after him.

It was the first time she could remember seeing him smile. It was the first time she could remember him speaking without first being

spoken to. It was the first time since his accident that he had allowed, let alone asked for, food to be prepared for him.

And something else. Something that wasn't her imagination.

She could have imagined the emptiness in the cottage, but there
was no mistaking the emptiness of Edward Garvey's eyes. Empty
windows, with nothing behind them. No emotion, no intelligence.
Nothing. The glass-marble eyes of a waxwork figure.

9

Darkness replaced moonlight as Harvey turned from watching the red speck of Peter's car dwindle into nothing. He glanced up at the sky, and the first spots of rain were cold on his face. Shivering, adjusting his scarf, he went to the front door, standing in the shelter of the tiny porch while he looked back over the black barrier of privet hedge at Rosemary's cottage.

He was tired, unusually so, and his head was starting to ache. The tensions of the evening. . . . He was in no condition to sit down and think. That would have to wait for tomorrow. Opening the door he went into the hall, switching on the light. Brass gleamed. The copper bowl of stocks on the tiny table glowed warmly. He turned unthinkingly to slide the bolt on the front door, a precaution he had never bothered about before. And then, when he realised what he had done, grimaced to himself, but still left the bolt as it was.

The place was silent. The door of the front room where Clive Murchison had spent nearly all his time since his arrival—sleeping on the couch—stood partly open. Harvey tugged pensively at his ear. He seemed to remember it had been closed when he had left the cottage earlier. But it wouldn't be the first time his lodger had foraged for food in his absence.

But there was something odd about the profound silence. Murchison, sleeping, had breathed noisily. Harvey pushed the door wider and took a step into the semi-darkness. He turned to feel for the switch and his foot came up against some obstruction that lay in the darkness of the floor. Then he found the switch and the room flooded with light. Murchison lay on his side on the floor, face turned to the ceiling, one arm thrown across his black-leather chest.

It was obvious, even before Harvey—throat suddenly tight—knelt at his side, that he was dead. The staring, sightless eyes told their own tale. The flesh, when he touched the forehead, was waxen-hard and ice-cold. But still, being who he was, he went through the motions, sliding one hand inside the white, frilled shirt to set his palm over the heart. And finding no life there he laid his fingers on the wrist, knowing there would be no pulse-throb to detect.

Rain spattered sharply against the window as he came slowly to his feet. For a moment his mind worked clearly. No sign of violence. Natural death. But it would mean a post-mortem. Which first—police or doctor?

Then shock came, and he fought against it, willing his body to stop shuddering, his hands to stop shaking, forcing all thoughts from his mind—and thoughts there were, a tumbling, racing torrent of them—except those of what must be done now.

A doctor first, to officially confirm death. Telephone. . . . The nearest one was at the farm.

Harvey stepped carefully over the body, hesitated, then stooped to close the lids with compassionate fingers. Switching off the light he went back into the hall, there to collect his raincoat, slipping it on while he made his way unhurriedly—haste at his age, no matter the circumstances, was a bad thing—along the passage, through the kitchen and out to the lean-to shed where he kept his bicycle.

The rain was coming down steadily now, pattering dismally on the corrugated-iron roof. The breeze whipped his coat between his legs. He turned on the bicycle lamp to show the way along the dark tree-tunnel at the side of the cottage. He was struggling with the wind-rocked gate, the light swinging, cutting golden swathes through the rain-filled darkness, when a voice called: "Harvey!" and Rosemary, coat held over her head, came running down the lane towards him.

He stopped with the bicycle half out of the gate, the wheel hard against his legs. Anxiety and impatience clashed to sharpen his voice.

"What's the matter?" And when she had reached his side: "Has something else happened?"

"Not like that." She shook her head under its cover. "It's Uncle Edward, Harvey. He came down and he spoke to me, and smiled. And he wanted me to get him something to eat. It's not like him. . . . And he's different." She laughed nervously, without humour. "Harvey, I think I'm frightened. . . ."

He finished manœuvring the bicycle into the lane to give himself time to think. He mustn't allow himself to get flustered. Which was more pressing?

"Where is he now?" he asked her.

"In the kitchen. Eating bacon and eggs. Eating!" Her laughter verged on hysteria. "As if he hadn't seen food in days. He asked for bacon and eggs, at this time of night."

Harvey reached a decision.

"Lock the door on him, Rosemary, just to be on the safe side. I don't think for a moment anything's wrong. I've got to go out—" He motioned vaguely, thankful that, preoccupied with her own worry, she hadn't apparently seen anything remarkable in his going out in the rain and so late at night. "I won't be long. As soon as I get back I'll come and look at him."

"All right." She started moving away. "Where are you going, Harvey?"

"Only to the farm." He adjusted the lamp that had been knocked askew. "A phone call I have to make."

There would be time enough later for explanations.

Mrs. Charnley, drawn by the opening of the front door, bustled from the kitchen. "Oh—It's you, Doctor," sounding surprised, as if she had been expecting someone else to come walking in at that time of night.

"It is," Peter replied, and went on without giving her space in which to insert curiosity. "Don't bother about getting me anything. I've had supper."

He had gone out without a coat. The dash from the garage after putting the car away had dampened his shoulders.

"Let me have your jacket," she said, "and I'll put it round the hot water tank."

When she had borne the jacket away he went into the surgery to consult the visiting-pad. No fresh names had been entered during the evening. There were only three visits on the agenda for the following morning.

Harvey Milton. . . . Leaning against the desk, his fingers groped for pockets that weren't there before he remembered that he had lost his jacket and his cigarettes.

He was worried about Harvey. The nonsense he had talked. . . . The mental meanderings of senility. But perhaps not, for the lapse had only been temporary, during the last few minutes before leaving. Then perhaps the after-effects of what, for an old man, must have been an exciting and upsetting evening. It had been nonsense; nothing of it had made sense. And then it seemed he must have been aware of it himself, for at the end he had tried to cover up the lapse. "If I were to tell you, you'd say I was out of my mind."

The phone rang and Peter picked up the receiver with one hand, a pen with the other, drawing a pad towards him with his elbow.

"Dr. Hill's surgery. The doctor speaking."

And a voice he recognised said steadily, without preamble: "Peter. You'd better come out here. It's Murchison. He's dead."

Peter stared at the receiver. "You're sure?"

Harvey sounded weary. "I'm sure."

"Murchison? According to you he was getting better. How did it happen? An accident?"

"I found him lying on the front room floor. It looked to me as if he'd struggled from the couch with the idea of getting to the door."

"Did you touch him at all?"

"Only enough to make sure he was dead. No one else knows yet. I suppose the police will have to be informed. I called you first."

"Don't call them until I've seen him for myself." It wouldn't be the first time a coma had been mistaken for death. "I'll be with you as soon as I can. Where are you calling from?"

"The farm. That's Betley Farm, the one by the bridge. I cycled here."

Peter looked at the window. The rain seemed to be coming down even more heavily.

"Hang on where you are," he said. "I'll pick you up. No sense in you getting more soaked than you must be already."

Mrs. Charnley was in the hall.

"Jacket, please," he said quickly. "An emergency. I don't know how long I'll be."

The head-on driving rain slowed his progress. It was fifteen minutes before the car rocked over the bridge. He slowed at the looming up of white-painted double gates, the door open ready for the huddled shape that came down the drive.

"It must have been a shock for you," he said accelerating.

Harvey leaned back, breathing heavily. "It was. I'm getting my second wind now. It was a shock. At one time I could have taken it in my stride and thought nothing of it." He seemed to be making conversation for the reassuring sound of his own steady voice. "During the war—the blitz—I was at a London school. I joined the Civil Defence—first aid, ambulance section. I became hardened to the sight of death in its various forms. Or as near hardened as one can get. But now, and in my own cottage. . . ."

The car skidded and Peter fought the wheel.

"It will mean the complications of a post-mortem and inquest," brooded Harvey. "I'm sorry I had to drag you in."

"All in a day's work. Does Rosemary know?"

"Rosemary. . . ." His passenger leaned forward. "I had almost forgotten. She came to see me just as I was leaving. She was worried about Edward, saying that he'd changed. But for the better, so far as I could make out. All the same, I told her to lock the door on him till I got back. For her peace of mind, that's all." He leaned back again. "I was tired to death before this started. Now I feel like I'll never sleep again."

Peter glanced anxiously sideways. In the dim light Harvey's face looked grey and lined.

"We'll soon have things sorted out," he promised. "Relax, try not to worry. I'll fix you up with something to make you sleep."

He would have driven past the cottage, not seeing it through the

84

rain and darkness, if Harvey hadn't tapped his shoulder. Heads sideways against the rain they hurried up the path.

"Here we are," Harvey said unnecessarily, fumbling with the latch and then pushing the door open. Inside he stopped abruptly, so that Peter, close behind, bumped into him in the darkness. There was a moment of confusion before the light came on—a heavy brass lantern, chain-hung at nearly head-level. It revealed Harvey's screwed-up mask of frowning perplexity.

"Is something wrong?" Peter asked quickly.

"I'm not certain; I'm trying to think." Harvey rubbed his forehead. "I never as a rule bolt the front door; I just leave it on the latch. But when I came in earlier I remember bolting it behind me and then wondering what had got into me. I'm sure I left it as it was —fastened. But it wasn't bolted now. . . ."

Peter nodded towards the closed door of the front room. "In there?"

"Yes." The old man pushed the door open. The dim, tinted light of the lantern wasn't sufficient to melt the darkness much beyond the threshold. He reached inside to find the switch. Peter blinked at the sudden brilliance. There was nothing to see. Apart from the usual furnishings the room was empty. There was certainly no body lying on the floor.

Edward Garvey finished eating, pushed the empty plates aside and sat back in his chair, hands folded placidly in his lap. His gaze travelled slowly round the room. He was able to recognise the things about him and find names for them.

This is the kitchen. That is the sink, that the stove, that the cupboard where the cups and saucers and plates are kept. Over the sink is the window. A window is for looking out on the outside. But not when it is dark. It is dark now, and raining.

There were other things he knew, instinctively, without the effort of remembering. He had been asleep. He had been awake and hungry. Now he had eaten and was no longer hungry. There was a pain in his leg, an ache in his side and his fingers were stiff and slow-moving. But they were bearable, and they were part of him, part of something called Edward Garvey. And he was feeling tired again.

When a man is hungry, he eats. When he is tired, he sleeps. A bed is used for sleeping. The bed is in the bedroom, which is upstairs.

He limped over to the door, but it refused to open. The handle turned, but the door was firm. When a door refuses to open, it is locked. When a door is locked and there is no key on the inside, then one has to ask for someone else to open the door.

"Rosemary?" called Edward Garvey.

It was a few moments before her voice came from the other side of the door. "Did you call, Uncle Edward?"

"I am tired. I would like to go to bed. The door is locked."

The key turned slowly, doubtfully, in the lock. The door opened.

"Thank you," he said politely, for it was right to offer thanks for a service. That was something he had been taught a long time ago. As he went past Rosemary he remembered something else. "Thank you for the food. It was very good."

He limped up the stairs. He closed the bedroom door behind him, but didn't turn the key in the lock. Neither did he inspect the room before undressing, putting on pyjamas and climbing between the cool sheets.

For the first time in many months he fell asleep immediately. For the first time in almost a year his rest was untroubled by dreams. There was a reason for that. Dreaming, like seeing, hearing, touching, is a sense associated with a faculty. A man with no eyes cannot see. A man whose ears are useless cannot hear. Edward Garvey didn't dream simply because he had lost that faculty.

"Perhaps," Peter said in the hall, "he's upstairs."

"No," Harvey said. "No." But all the same he followed Peter from room to room. It was a tour that didn't take very long. Back in the front room he stooped, grunted a little, to turn on the small electric fire that stood on the white-tiled hearth.

"Not all that warm," he commented, straightening.

"No," Peter said.

"I'm not a fool," the other said. "He was dead."

"A coma can often be mistaken for death. Even experts make mistakes."

"No," said Harvey, "not a coma," and started to rebutton his rain-coat.

"I'll come with you," Peter said.

Harvey, reaching for his belt, looked up. "I'm not going out there to look for him. I'm going over to see Edward."

"That's what I thought. I'd better come with you."

"One thing on top of another," said the ex-schoolmaster tonelessly. "No, I'd better go alone. Rosemary would wonder why you were here. I couldn't very well tell her I'd sent for you on account of her uncle. I don't want to tell her the real reason."

"No," Peter agreed.

"If anything is wrong, anything at all, I'll come right back for you."

Left alone, Peter took off his coat, folded it and laid it over the back of a chair. The room was beginning to warm up. The fire couldn't have been used for some time, there was the faint smell of burning dust.

He had an idea that Murchison was a diabetic. That would certainly explain his earlier collapse, the state in which Harvey first found him. But it didn't explain his disappearance now. Diabetics who fall into a coma don't normally recover without outside assistance. There was the possibility though, that Murchison had come round sufficiently to realise what was happening and had managed to give himself an insulin injection. But that was unlikely, and didn't explain why he had afterwards left the place.

There were other possibilities. . . . Epilepsy was one. The only certain thing was that Harvey had mistaken unconsciousness for death. Dead bodies don't get up and walk away. And no one was likely to have come into the place and carried it away.

There was the sound of the front door opening. Harvey had been away only a few minutes. Peter met him in the hall.

"Is everything all right?"

Removing his now saturated coat the other nodded. "At least that's one little problem out of the way. Edward's gone back to bed again. I went up to see for myself. He was fast asleep."

In the front room Harvey opened the door of the sideboard cupboard and after some searching produced a small bottle of whisky.

"Kept for medicinal purposes." He put it on the table. "Too expensive a luxury for pleasure."

"In hot water," Peter told him. "A good stiff dose. Probably help you sleep better than the stuff I had in mind."

"You'll join me, of course?" the other invited from the door on his way to the kitchen.

The bottle was a new one, untouched, and there was the long drive back through the rain.

"It's an idea," Peter said.

Harvey returned from the kitchen with two tumblers, poured spirit into each and replaced the cork with studied care.

"It wasn't a coma," he told it. "I've worked in hospitals. Reception. We got all sorts. I know death when I see it." He looked up. "Murchison was cold. He'd been dead for some time."

A distant whistling sent him hurrying kitchenwards again. He returned with kettle in one hand, sugar-basin in the other. Peter accepted his glass, sipped it, found it too hot and set it on the mantelpiece. Harvey made to seat himself on the couch, grimaced, changed his mind and drew a hard-backed chair up to the fire. He cradled his glass between stubby fingers.

"You'd better tell me exactly what happened," Peter said.

"There's not much you don't already know. I came back in the cottage and bolted the door behind me. And I'm positive now I left it that way. I went out the back way for my bicycle. I came in here, it was dark, stumbled over something. . . ." He pointed one finger without unclasping his hands. "He was just inside. Fully dressed; he used to sleep that way; his idea, not mine. My impression was that he'd managed to get as far as the door and then collapsed. And died."

"Did you ever see him using a hypodermic syringe, or taking medicine of any kind?"

"Diabetes," Harvey said. "That was the first thing I thought of when he collapsed in my arms out there in the lane. I even made a point of smelling his breath. No trace of acetone. I've met diabetic comas before."

He studied the steaming contents of his glass.

"I did all the things you or any other doctor would have done.

God knows I've been through the routine often enough before, even if I lacked the luxury of a stethoscope. He wasn't breathing. I checked heart and pulse. I closed his eyes. I would say he had been dead for at least an hour."

He had spoken calmly and deliberately, using the oddly convincing tone of one who is sure of himself and doesn't particularly care whether his listener believes him or not. It brought Peter to the brink of acceptance.

But if Murchison was dead, where was his body now?

Harvey said steadily: "The front door was bolted on the inside. I locked the back door behind me when I left for the farm. It's still locked; the key's in my pocket. No one could have entered the cottage."

"The body came back to life," Peter said bleakly. "It opened the front door and stalked into the darkness. Is that what you're trying to say?"

"Can you think of anything else?" the other asked evenly.

And some time later, as they stood in the porch, with the rain over and the moon trying to break through the clouds, Harvey said:

"We can't do anything about it. Not officially, you know. You must see that. We can't take a story like this to authority. The police, even of the rural variety, aren't that credulous. And they have a penchant for attaching labels. And labels of that kind have a habit of sticking."

Peter knew what he meant. "But we can't just leave things as they are. . . ."

"I don't see that there's anything we can do," said the older man simply. "Not as things stand at the moment."

"I suppose not," Peter said helplessly, and looked in the direction of the hills. "He was making for those. . . . But we can't start looking out there for him."

"Murchison is dead," said Harvey.

"Tomorrow," Peter told him. "I'll get out here again as early as I can tomorrow. Perhaps by then—" He broke off.

"At least we should both be in better shape to work things out after a night's sleep," Harvey said.

Peter walked to his car. With his hand on the door he turned to look in the direction of Greymill Cottage. All the windows were in darkness.

Rosemary was asleep. So was Edward Garvey. And so, strangely enough, lying on the dry soil floor of a cave, was Argred the Freeman.

10

The sun, topping the hills at the far side of the valley, rising into the almost cloudless sky of a new day, flooded the shallow cave with warm brilliance. The man who lay there, sprawled on the soft soil floor, hands clasped behind his neck, stirred, not yet fully awake, not opening his eyes, stretching his legs luxuriously like some basking animal.

After a while he opened his eyes. A rock ceiling swam into focus. His gaze moved downwards. Uneven rocky walls; a pile of rubble near the wide entrance; a bush silhouetted against a clear blue sky. Thoughts came slowly with returning awareness.

He was Argred the Freeman. The pain and weariness had gone. He was in a cave that was little more than a scooped hollow. The light—he narrowed his eyes—was much brighter than usual. But that would be because he had slept so long in the caverns of the Old People. And the air here was sharper, fresher; and that too could be because of the days spent in the stale dead air of the caves.

Coming to his feet he went to stand in the entrance, shielding his eyes against the glare while he gazed around in wonderment.

Where is this place? he asked inside his mind.

Describe it, whispered a voice.

It is a place I have never seen before. Everything is strange.

You are in another man's body, the voice told him. *You are seeing through another man's eyes. There will be strangeness for a while.*

Could different eyes make light so much brighter? Could different nostrils make the air so much sweeter?

I am standing in the entrance to a cave, thought Argred. There are other caves on either side. The ground slopes away in front; grass, bushes, trees, distant hills. . . .

He stepped into the open, turning, looking behind, upwards.

There are hills behind. No mountains. . . .

And then panic, for all through his life his horizons had been dominated by the towering pinnacles of the mountains. No matter how far a man might travel the mountains were always there. Now they were gone.

Where am I? he asked.

We can only see through your mind, the voice told him.

There is a fence and a gate at the foot of the slope, Argred said inside his mind. A road that winds away. There are two dwelling places, one with a roof of dried grass, the other, some kind of red stone. Far away are the roofs of more buildings, but there is mist about them.

Dwelling places, echoed the voice warningly. *Be careful. You must not be seen.*

Where are the mountains? implored Argred.

The voice was silent.

He held out his hands. The narrow palms and tapering fingers of a stranger. Kolda's hands. And these, Kolda's legs.

He stared down at his legs, wondering at the thin blue fabric that clung tightly about them, reaching down to touch it, feeling the dampness, remembering then the darkness and the rain. . . . And remembering too that Kolda had worn no covering on his legs and feet. Argred lifted one foot, marvelling at its case of hard black leather, fashioned and stitched into shape, fastened with laced cords.

And the jacket. Not the uncured leather of the plains, gathered with thongs at breast and waist, but smooth, satisfying to the touch, with fastenings of round pieces of bone.

Argred's hands lifted to feel the matted luxuriance of hair. Kolda's hair. And Kolda's high-boned nose and arrogant, jutting chin. This was Kolda's body. But these weren't Kolda's clothes.

Where am I? he asked inside his mind. What has happened to me?

He had lain, dying, on the floor of the Place of the Machines. Marna had crouched like some dusty vulture. Kolda had slept at his side.

It will take a little time, the voices warned. *When you wake again you will be in Kolda's body. But there will be nothing of Kolda left. Your thoughts will be your own, but linked with ours. You will be one with our wisdom. You will know how to find the hidden tools. You will know how to use them to make weapons.*

We are ready, whispered the voices. *Sleep. . . .*

He had slept.

And then the awakening. But not to the white brilliance and hard floor of the Place of the Machines.

Instead—darkness, with a softness between his body and the ground. With a voice inside his head shouting a silent warning of danger. There were shapes dimly visible in the darkness. And the emptiness of a doorway. Hands groping he went through it, meeting a barrier that was not a rock, with the voice shouting still. His hands touched strange, invisible objects and projections. Another barrier, and his hands told him it was a door. They found a bolt and slid it aside. The door opened towards him.

Darkness still, but now there was moving air and rain on his face. Danger in front, warned the silent voice of his new instinct; danger to the right. The door pressed against his shoulders, sucked by the wind. He heard it close as he moved in the direction of no danger. There were no moons, no stars, but facing him, where safety lay, he could discern the outlines of low, rolling hills.

To reach them meant thrusting through bushes, crossing a narrow open place where the sodden ground dragged at his feet, then forcing a way through more bushes, these growing close together, branches raking his face and hands. Then open, sloping ground with unsuspected hollows.

The warning cry faded. The slope became steeper. Gusts of wind drove rain-lances into his face. There was no way of telling how long he climbed. A dark towering mass became a rock face. He groped along it, finding the opening—a cave that offered shelter and dryness. He felt his way along its wall. When he reached the end and so could go no further he threw himself to the ground and fell asleep.

That had been last night. This was the morning of a new day, of a new life. His new body was unscarred, untouched by pain. Hunger suddenly gnawed.

Smoke curled lazily from one of the dwellings below. Smoke meant fire; a fire, someone to light it; an occupant meant food. But a man who wishes his presence to remain unknown doesn't forage on his own threshold. Near the place where there was a bridge—and a bridge meant water—the dark roofs of buildings floated above the drifting mist. Far enough away not to attract attention to a hiding place in the hills; near enough for a first foray in this strange country.

But first, his new instinct told him, he must find another place of concealment. A larger cave than this, one that bites deeply into the rock, with perhaps the luxury of nearby drinking-water. One with a level dry floor and an entrance that can be protected. A place to which the tools of the Old People can be brought, assembled and put to use.

There were only four patients in the waiting-room, all with only trivial complaints. Late starting, for he had overslept—and so also had Mrs. Charnley, her compressed lips a constant reminder that she had waited up for him last night—Peter had dealt with them by ten-fifteen. He was drinking coffee and entering records when Mr. Brownlee appeared.

"I'm not too late, Doc?" he asked, eying the cup.

"You're all right. And how's that hand of yours?"

"Loads better. I wouldn't 'ave come worryin' you again only I've 'eard I'm due to go on nights an' I wanted the all clear first."

"It sounds as if you don't mind working nights."

Brownlee added a knowing wink to his grin. "Extra pay and only a bit of maintenance to see to. Which means the odd 'and of solo with the guards. There's four on nights; two off, two on."

Peter removed the dressing. The inflammation had gone and there were already signs of healthy granulation.

"You should be able to cope with a hand of cards," he said dryly.

"And don't go poking your nose again into things that don't concern you."

"I won't, Doc," the patient assured him fervently.

No more names had been added to the three on the visiting list. By quarter to eleven Peter had disposed of them and was on his way to Betley Hatch. Harvey, looking surprisingly none the worse for his previous night's experience, leaned on his gate smoking his pipe. His silver hair gleamed elegantly; there was even a rose in his buttonhole.

"Pleasant after the rain," he greeted Peter with genial triteness. "Did you sleep well?"

"You look cheerful enough," Peter remarked with small resentment.

"Worrying never got anyone anywhere. A lesson I learnt a long time ago." Harvey knocked out his pipe against his heel. "Slept like a top. The whisky, I suppose."

"So nothing else has happened?"

"I wouldn't say that. First things first. Right now, Edward's taking himself for a walk. It's the first time he's been outside the cottage since his accident. I had a short chat with him. One thing's certain, Peter; he's changed. He's a different man. Bear that in mind. . . ."

He scratched his nose with the pipe-stem.

"I had a visit from our local police sergeant earlier this morning. It appears there's been a spot of trouble down at Betley Farm. Someone broke in during the night or early morning and took food and a transistor radio belonging to the farmer's daughter—Crabley's his name. All the police have to go on is a set of foot-prints made with pointed shoes of the type I believe are much favoured by the younger generation." He paused. "Along with leather jackets and jeans. Sergeant Rowntree came to see if either Rosemary or I had seen any strangers knocking about recently."

"So you told him about Murchison," Peter said tonelessly.

Harvey shook his head.

"No, I didn't. Rowntree is an estimable man and knows his job. But he's not possessed of a stretchable imagination. If I had told him of last night's events he would have jumped to the only conclusion that Murchison must have recovered while I was away phoning. And then, of course, he would have wanted to know why you hadn't done anything about a sick man on the loose."

"I should never have let myself—" Peter started, and then clamped his mouth on angry self-admonition.

"I know. You're blaming yourself for having allowed me to persuade you against your better judgment. But I'm not going back on anything I said last night. I want to talk to you about that. But first, there's something I want to show you."

Taking Peter's arm he led him a few paces along the path, pointing with his pipe.

"Those bushes. . . . See the freshly-broken branches?" He dropped to his haunches, pulling Peter with him. "Foot-print in the soil. Pointed shoe. There's a trail of them the other side, leading to the hedge. And there's a gap in the hedge where someone forced a way through."

He came grunting to his feet.

"Murchison came out of the cottage and instead of keeping to the path, turned to plough his way through the garden, making a bee-line for the hills. I would guess he found shelter in one of the caves. And when he got hungry he raided the farm in search of food. Now he's probably back in the hills again."

"Murchison," Peter said heavily.

"Who else?"

"A deal of activity for a man who is supposed to be dead."

Harvey took his arm again. "Come inside and let me tell you all about it."

The couch had been pushed back against the wall. Harvey sat on a well-worn leather easy chair with his legs crossed, his hands clasped, thumbs uppermost, in his lap. He regarded Peter with the wisely benevolent gaze of a schoolmaster having a parting talk with a pupil of school-leaving age.

"You will have to bear with me," he started. "It's a long story and it had its beginnings many years ago. For a while it won't make any sense to you."

Peter, seated in the matching chair at the other side of the fireplace, took out cigarettes and lighter.

"Nothing," he commented briefly, "makes sense right now."

"It does to me," Harvey said. "I think it will to you. At first sight it seems incredible, but all the pieces fit, and there is an answer, a reason.

"It starts some forty years ago when I was a fairly young man and very conscious of my first important position as Latin and English Master at a suburban Grammar School. With youthful revolutionary ideas about applied education, I was hampered by the old-fashioned ideas of the headmaster and limited by the text-books available. One of my pupils was a not over-bright boy named Jeremy Ferguson. He is now Sir Jeremy Miles-Ferguson, a Harley Street consultant psychiatrist. But that is by the way. . . .

"A Latin class, then, with Master Ferguson paying more attention to something on his lap than to me. I confiscated from him a lurid, over-coloured periodical of the type popularly referred to as a 'comic'. An American import, it was called, I remember, *Spaceways*.

"Retributory punishment being called for, I sought something that would fit the crime and also be of a constructive nature. I ordered the culprit to translate the text of the front page of illustrations into Latin. When he presented his effort to me the following morning I was agreeably surprised. But then the writer of the original text had employed a style little removed from basic English, and the subject matter was of a juvenile nature. I saw the possibilities. Most of the boys in the class already took the comic regularly. From my own resources I bought copies for those that didn't.

"For the remainder of that term I taught Latin with the aid of a serial from the comic and the standard text-books. The terminal examination results were very gratifying. Unfortunately the Head came to hear of my experiment and, despite its success, put an end to it."

Harvey paused with the air of one on the verge of a denouement.

"You are asking yourself what all this can possibly have to do with Clive Murchison and Edward Garvey. Let me give you a connection. The particular story my pupils and I dealt with concerned the adventures of one Argred the Freeman whose home was on the planet Andrida."

11

Sunlight, slanting through the narrow window, spilled warmly across Peter's legs. He sought for some comment to offer Harvey's air of expectancy, failed and moved irritably, ash flaking from his cigarette to spill unheeded down the front of his jacket.

"Argred the Freeman," Harvey said, spacing his words carefully. "The name that Mrs. Cookson mentioned. Also in the story was a woman called Rhoweena, and that was the name Rosemary heard her uncle use."

"A story from a child's comic?" Peter didn't know whether to be annoyed or amused.

"I know." The other nodded. "Arrant nonsense. An impossible association. That's how I felt at first; that's why I needed time to think before telling you. But hear me out, Peter, before you ridicule. This is something in three—no, four parts. The first is what I've just told you; the link, for Edward must have read that story when he was a child, and although he has probably forgotten it, his subconscious hasn't. Then comes the story itself, and you will have to bear with me while I tell you that. Then there is the thing that happened last night, and finally, the events that are taking place now.

"The story itself, then. . . ." Harvey stared down at his clasped hands. "Hardly what one might call a literary gem. The anonymous author had made use of every stock situation with a scant regard for verisimilitude. One received the impression that he had dealt out the various stages like playing-cards from a pack, or from a list tacked for reference above his typewriter. He had included everything; mind-rays, torture, underground places filled with mummies, poison, strange machines, magic—the lot. But the story was, of course, only intended for a juvenile readership.

"It had been running for some months before I happened upon it, but there was a synopsis of past episodes. The scene, as you already know, was a mythical world called Andrida—and I can recall the writer's words—a faraway planet, a million light years away, somewhere on the dark lonely fringes of the Galaxy. . . ."

Peter's cigarette burned down and he collected an ashtray from the mantelpiece. After a while he lighted a second cigarette, watching Harvey's impassive features first over the flame of his lighter and then through the blue haze of smoke.

"And that," Harvey concluded, "is where end of term found us, with Argred, now in Kolda's body, out in the open again, busy assembling the tools and beginning to realise that something was happening to him. My own impression was that it was a narrative designed to drag on for as long as the editor of the periodical was prepared to use it."

Peter stubbed out his cigarette.

"I read much the same sort of stuff when I was a boy," he said. "Garvey may have read that particular story—by the sound of it, he did. But I still don't see what you're driving at."

"You will." Harvey nodded. "But before moving on, let us consider certain parallels. Edward has made enemies of doctors in general; Argred's enemies were the Mind-Healers. Argred suffered pain as the result of torture; Edward's is the result of his accident. Argred was poisoned; up until last night Edward's phobia made him prepare all his own food because he was afraid of being poisoned. Kolda's description, even to the black leather jacket, fits Murchison perfectly. And they both came to a strange place under some kind of compulsion.

"There are other parallels if one looks for them. Rosemary and Rhoweena. Mrs. Cookson could be Marna the Wisewoman. You are one of the Mind-Healers. I suppose I could step into Old Lorr's shoes. Two series of events and people, one fictional, one real, running side by side and matching to an astonishing degree."

"By stretching imagination to an astonishing degree as well," Peter said.

"Not so much as you would think. But we'll forget that for the time being. Let's talk about Edward for a while. More or less for all his life he's suffered from a form of persecution mania. He read that story long ago for much the same reason we all read stories, a temporary escape from the world of reality. He identified himself, as the author intended, with the main character. For a little while he lived Argred's life. And as he grew up, so he forgot the story. But it was still in his subconscious mind. You can't argue with that."

"No," Peter said doubtfully.

"After his accident, as you know, his condition worsened. He became completely at loggerheads with the world of reality. His subconscious delved into the past to present him with a means of escape. Perhaps the parallels were the stimulus. In his dreams he lived Argred's existence in the caverns of the Lost Moon. The fact that he called out Rhoweena's name in the moment of waking is proof of this. His subconscious brought Argred to life. . . ."

Harvey paused. "And at the first opportunity, using yet another parallel, it put life into a dead body. Only the new life, of course, was a completely different one from the original."

Peter stared at him incredulously. "You don't know what you're saying. . . ."

"There is nothing supernatural about it," Harvey said calmly. "Not when you come to consider. Schizophrenia taken to its ultimate logical extreme. There were two—what?—beings inside Edward's mind; himself and Argred. One was his normal, thinking mind; the other his subconscious. All that has happened is that the subconscious being has left him, taking up occupancy in a suitable vehicle.

"It's nothing new. The 'possession' of the Middle Ages—to be possessed of an evil spirit. Hypnotism is another facet. One person's mind temporarily controls the body of another. And reincarnation. . . . A large slice of the world's population implicitly believes that the life-essence, the soul, leaves the dying body to take up residence in a new body. And many psychiatrists believe that the soul is merely another name for the subconscious."

Peter had to force his voice to match the evenness of the other's.

"Let me get this straight. What you are suggesting is that Garvey's mind split completely and that part of it—the personality of Argred—moved to occupy Murchison's dead body."

"The third part of my story," Harvey said; "the thing that happened last night, triggered off, I feel sure, by the parallel of Mrs. Cookson's presence. According to her the cottage was filled with a presence. What she was sensing was the essence as it were of Edward's subconscious, groping blindly between existence and non-existence, causing in the process the poltergeistic disturbances. Growing pains"—he made a gesture—"one could call them that. And then she declared that something had happened, that the presence had gone.

"There is a small confusion of time. . . . I think that, for a while, the presence existed in a kind of no man's time. Murchison was lying dead. Whether or not his death was natural is something we'll probably never know. But in due course his body was taken over by Argred the Freeman, and Edward woke up, minus his subconscious, and consequently, a vastly changed man."

There was a silence. Harvey produced pipe and pouch and became busy with them. Peter, not knowing what he was doing, lighted yet another cigarette and went over to the window, looking out at the hills but not seeing anything.

"It has to eat," came Harvey's dispassionate voice. "That's why it broke into the farm—to get food. There's something odd about that break-in, but we'll leave it for the time being. You'll have enough on your plate. Think about it. You'll have to do that. All the pieces fit. . . ."

The silence again. Through the smell of his cigarette Peter caught the sweet pungency of the tobacco Harvey used.

"If you get the chance," came his voice again, "talk to Edward. It's a pity you didn't know him before. But you'll certainly find something very strange about him without need of comparison. Empty—a sleep-walker awake. Will you tell your uncle about all this?"

"Uncle Andrew?" Peter took a deep breath. "No. No, I don't think so."

"A pity," sighed Harvey. "But perhaps you'll change your mind when you've had time to think. I hope you do. I have the feeling we're going to need all the help we can get."

Peter drove back towards Colford, slowly, forgetting even to change gear, the car moving at little more than a walking pace. The horror that coiled at the back of his mind he refused to acknowledge, thrusting it deliberately away, trying to cancel it with mental repudiation of Harvey's theory. For it was a theory, wildly impossible, and nothing more. Facts distorted and twisted to fit events. Reason insisted upon that.

Deep in thought, features set, hands flat on the wheel, he passed without paying attention to a man who came plodding steadily along the lane in the direction of Betley. And then he braked sharply and turned to look back through the rear window. An elderly man wearing an ill-fitting grey jacket and not over-clean flannels. A man with thinning colourless hair who carried himself erect but had the stiff marionette gait of a sleep-walker. It had to be Edward Garvey.

Turning back to the wheel, Peter released the brake and moved on. He stopped again when he came abreast of the white gates of Betley Farm. A stocky man wearing mud-splashed breeches and leather gaiters was crossing the yard, a black and white dog at his heels. At sight of the car he hesitated and then came towards the gate.

Peter wound down the window to lean out.

"I'm sorry," he apologised lamely as the farmer rested tweed-covered arms along the top of the gate. "I didn't mean to interrupt. My name is Hill, Dr. Hill."

"Crabley," nodded the farmer. "I fancied I recognised the car. Likely you've been up to see old Garvey. How's that sister of his getting on?"

Peter had to think for a moment. "She's coming along nicely." He nodded in the direction of the slate-roofed sprawling farmhouse. "I hear you've had a spot of trouble."

"News gets round." Mr. Crabley lifted a grizzled moustache in a yellow-toothed grimace. "The first thing like that we've had since I've been farming the place. It's got Rowntree running round in circles." The grimace became a grin. "You met the local sergeant yet?"

"Not yet."

"He's what you might call baffled. A vagrant, he says. But it weren't no ordinary tramp. I'll stake my boots on that." His pause was significance itself.

"What makes you think that?" Peter asked steadily.

"Figure it out for yourself. Last night the wife says she needs new curtains. All right, so I gives her eight quid and she puts it on the dresser in the kitchen with the daughter's radio on top. I get up this morning at my usual time of quarter after five, and like always, I go across to the shippen. The wife comes down half an hour later, and it has to be during that half hour that the stuff's taken. I reckon the cheeky sod must've been waiting, sees me crossing the yard and then nips in smartish. Takes a hunk of dry bread and a hunk of cheese that had seen better days. Leaves a plate of cooked sausages and some bars of chocolate—doesn't touch them. Pops into the kitchen and helps himself to the radio—"

Crabley paused for the climax.

"And leaves the eight quid. He takes a broken radio, and anyone could see it was broke, and leaves the money behind when he must have seen it. Now I ask you, what bloody tramp—or anyone else in their right mind for that matter—would pinch a few bits of dried grub and a broken radio, and leave good food and eight quid behind?"

"It doesn't seem to make sense," Peter said in a voice he didn't recognise as his own.

"You're damned right it doesn't. I only called in the police because he was so damned cheeky. There's another thing. Sheila here"—the dog set its front paws on the farmer's chest at mention of its name—"I've had her a good few years now. Afraid of nothing. Sleeps in the barn. I let her out in the morning and she comes back with me for a bite of breakfast. But not this morning. She comes with me as far as the door, then down goes her nose, up comes her hackles and she's tearing back to the barn as if all the devils in hell are on her tail. And now she won't go anywhere near the house."

The dog dropped back to the ground to stand, tongue lolling, tail tucked tightly away, gazing up into her master's face.

"She's only ever acted like that once before," Crabley mused; "a long time back. She went into the parlour where my old father was, turned round and belted out. Only he was dead in his coffin. They say dogs can smell death. So I've heard." His moustache twisted to his grin. "But a dead bloke wouldn't be interested in bread and cheese. I reckoned he'd been somewhere—a mortuary or such-like—and brought the smell with him. I mentioned it to Rowntree but he didn't seem impressed."

"You're probably right," Peter said with an effort, and reached for the starter. The car rocked over the hump-backed bridge. At the Southam fork he pulled into the side of the road, stopped, rested his elbows on the wheel and stared hard for quite some time at a clump of trees. And then, for all it was nearly one o'clock, he turned the car to face back in the direction of Betley.

Harvey took a few moments to answer his knock. He was in shirt sleeves. There was a tea-towel pinned about his waist and a can-opener in one hand.

"I didn't expect to see you again so soon, Peter." But his voice held little surprise. He led the way to the tiny kitchen. On the table were a half loaf, a small bowl of butter and a cup and saucer. A frying pan on the stove held a solitary rasher of bacon. A can of baked beans, the lid only partly cut through, explained the can-opener. Despite the turmoil of his thoughts Peter still found something pathetic in the ingredients of the lonely meal.

Harvey spread apologetic hands. "I'm afraid I can't ask you to join me. . . ." There was no embarrassment, only a quiet dignity.

Peter said: "What are we going to do about all this?"

Harvey laid the can-opener on the table. "I can't tell you how pleased I am to hear the collective pronoun. I had never felt so alone in my life before. What made you change your mind?"

Peter told him of his encounter with Crabley.

The other grinned wryly. "Sausages and chocolate. An odd fulcrum on which to balance your lever of decision. Argred didn't take them, of course, because sausages and chocolate aren't mentioned in the story. Bread, meat and cheese are. Or was it the dog's instinct that gave you second thoughts?"

Peter shook his head impatiently. "That's not important."

"No. And you ask what are we going to do about it. There's very little we can do. I've had longer to think about it than you. We're agreed that there's something up in the hills that isn't human. Virtually a being from another planet, an alien. But who would believe that a character from a story could come to life and occupy a human body?"

"We can't tell anyone that; not unless we want to be labelled as insane. It wouldn't make any difference if you had seen Murchison for yourself and verified he was dead. We can't tell the police he was in a coma, recovered and wandered off into the night, because then they would want to know why you hadn't reported the matter. Dead ends, Peter; we're on our own."

"But we can't leave things like this!" Peter exclaimed angrily. "This is—" He stopped. "Does Rosemary know anything about all this?"

"Not yet. After the police had been I did debate with myself whether or not to tell her about my lodger. I decided not to. But she may have to be told the whole story." Harvey touched the can-opener, making it swivel. "She may have to leave her cottage. And giving a reason, I would rather tell her the truth than invent a lie."

Peter sat down heavily. "You think she may be in danger?"

"No more so than the rest of us. My knowledge of the story ends with Argred, in his new body, getting ready to avenge himself on his enemies. I have no way of knowing if Rhoweena, who poisoned him, was singled out for special treatment."

Harvey paused.

"You won't have had time to appreciate the full significance of what is happening or is going to happen. We can forget that Clive Murchison ever existed. He is dead in every sense of the word. To all intents and purposes the man out there is Argred the Freeman. He is living an existence invented and set down on paper by some writer forty years ago, and stored in Edward's mind until yesterday. I believe his new life will follow the fictional one. Argred's sole purpose, in the story, was to destroy his enemies. And he had come to believe that everyone was his enemy."

Peter looked at the window. He could see down the back garden; neat rows of peas, more of beans, lines of seedlings. There was the privet hedge, and beyond, the green and purple folds of the hills.

"Even after the farm," he said dazedly, "even after that, I still can't bring myself to accept all this."

"I suppose," Harvey said equably, "it is easier for me than you. My life was lived in a world of books. I've existed out here, in the wilds and virtually alone, for a goodly few years. One easily gets out of step with the outside, everyday world. So when something like this happens along it isn't too difficult to accept it."

"I have accepted part of it. Persecution mania developing into schizophrenia. That's reasonable. But the rest. . . . And now to suggest that the story will go on from where it left off—"

"It is already going on," Harvey said quietly. "Stealing the food wasn't significant. Taking the transistor was. In the story the Old People had provided him with the instinct of where to find the tools. They were pictured in the illustration as pieces of electronic equipment. Now do you see?"

"I don't see," Peter replied stubbornly. "You're trying to apply reason to something beyond reason. You can't make something out of nothing. Argred was created by a writer who made up the tools out of his head as he went along. They have no basis in fact. They can't be turned into reality."

"An example," said Harvey. "A subject under hypnosis can be made to speak in French when he has no knowledge of the language. Much the same sort of thing, only on a much larger scale, is happening now. Murchison's mind and body has become completely occupied by the essence of Argred the Freeman. In his mind is the knowledge of the Old People. As I told you, I only know the story as far as the point where Argred was starting to assemble the tools for making weapons, and was just becoming aware of a change that was taking place in himself. What that change was, of course, I have no idea, but it was caused by exposure to sunlight after the presumably radio-active emanations of the glowing fungus, a stroke of inspired prophecy on the writer's part. Was radioactivity known of forty years ago?"

"I don't know," Peter said dully.

"It would be useless trying to find him," Harvey said. "There are some ten miles of hills and parts of them are riddled with caves, most of them unexplored. And even if we did by chance happen on the right one, his instinct would warn him of our approach.

"But there is something we can do. The original story must have an ending. We can try to find out what that ending is, and the events leading up to it. Forewarned is forearmed. Tomorrow morning—today being early-closing for the shops—I intend to visit each of the Colford newsagents in turn in the hope that one of them may have records going back forty years. If we can discover who the importers of the magazine were we should be able to contact the publishers, and through them, the writer. If he's still alive. And that's all we can do."

It was two o'clock when Peter arrived back at the surgery. He offered apology but no explanation to Mrs. Charnley, suffering the oven-spoiled meal without complaint, hardly tasting the food as it passed his lips. In the surgery itself he found that six names were on the afternoon visiting list. He was checking the contents of his case when Mrs. Charnley ushered in a policeman.

The young, pink-cheeked constable, helmet tucked under arm, was apologetic.

"I'm sorry to trouble you, sir; I won't keep you a moment."

Peter closed the case and rested his hands on the top.

"And what can I do for you, Constable?"

It seemed that the rural police were more astute than either Mr. Crabley or Harvey had given them credit for.

"Just a routine enquiry, sir. We're trying to trace the movements of a young man, a stranger to the district. Age about twenty; tall, long fair hair; wearing a black leather jacket and blue jeans. No hat."

Peter's hands tightened on the handle of the case. "And you think I may have seen him?"

"Not you in particular, sir. We're checking with everyone whose work entails driving regularly about the district. This young man is known to have spent most of Sunday on a bench on the forecourt of the Memorial Hospital. He was seen later in the day on the Southam road, trying to hitch a lift from passing cars. We are anxious to find out if he did manage to get a lift, or if he is still likely to be in the locality."

Peter swung his case from the desk in a gesture implying dismissal.

"I'm afraid I'm one of those people who drive automatically, Constable. I keep an eye on the traffic and see very little else."

"Yes, sir." The visitor adjusted his helmet, paying particular attention to the chin-strap. "That's what most of them say. One of them told me he wouldn't even notice Lady Godiva unless her horse happened to get in his way."

The round of visits kept Peter occupied until half past four. Evening surgery, with an almost full waiting-room, took him to seven-fifteen. The phone rang as he was entering up the last record card. Its message, from one of the local midwives, was of a premature confinement that could, in her words, prove a mite tricky.

After a quick drive out along the Banbury road he spent the remainder of the evening dividing his time between drinking over-brewed tea in a candle-lit kitchen and sitting at the bedside of the middle-aged farmer's wife in a tiny attic room lighted with all the oil-lamps her anxious husband possessed. It was almost midnight before he was able to climb wearily into his car and head for home.

And about the same time, Argred the Freeman was standing at the entrance to his new cave—a cave that twisted deeply into the side of a hill—looking out over the darkened valley.

He had eaten the food and now was in need of more. Finding it with his new cunning would be easy. The need wasn't urgent, and that was strange. Bread and cheese is little enough to keep a man in strength for a day. He was hungry, but not famished. There was no urgency. But there was an urgency to the clamour of the silent voices, urging him, ordering him to search for the tools so that the weapons could be made.

There is little time, they said. *Go, now.* . . .

There is all the time I need, he told them proudly. I have nothing to fear in this place, of these people.

Go! they commanded.

He obeyed, leaving the cave, clambering down the scree of tumbled rock, wading through the shallow, frothing stream, making his way towards the fields and the houses and the town beyond.

12

Mrs. Charnley brought the news of the second burglary with the mid-morning coffee and biscuits. As was usual with the tit-bits of local gossip she so avidly garnered, it had come to her already much added to, and she augmented it still further in the latest telling.

"Hawson's in Colford Road, Doctor. You know the shop—televisions and washing-machines. Ransacked during the night. The police are looking for a gang with a lorry."

Harvey, arriving just as Peter had emptied the waiting-room and was preparing for his morning rounds, brought the more accurate version. But then he had made it his business to talk with the manager of the pillaged shop.

Peter, who had been tired to the point of exhaustion after the previous day's finale of the protracted farmhouse delivery and who had as a result slept soundly, was more his usual self. He had also had time to consider the implications of the latest burglary.

"My private Gestapo has already brought the news," he said. "A gang using a lorry, she tells me." And at the patent disappointment on his visitor's face at not being the one to bring the news: "But knowing Mrs. Charnley I expect her version is exaggerated."

Harvey sank into a chair, took the handkerchief from his breast pocket, wiped his forehead and adjusted his rose-bud buttonhole.

"A shop selling electrical equipment," Peter observed during the proceedings. "More transistors?"

"Not this time," Harvey told him. "But much the same pattern.

No foot-prints left behind, but apparently the police have a nice set of what the manager called 'dabs'. By which I assume he means finger prints. I don't think they'll find them of much use. Unless Murchison had a record. A possibility, that." He fingered his bottom lip thoughtfully.

"What did he take this time?"

"He operated in the workshop at the back of the shop. A small television set is missing, and a carton of dry batteries of the kind called power-packs. There was a cupboard containing odds and ends of food, but all he took was a half-loaf and a shrivelled piece of boiled ham. He also helped himself to a number of tools; pliers, screwdrivers and an electric soldering iron. And some rolls of cable and an assortment of television parts that happened to be lying around on one of the benches.

"On the same shelf from which the batteries were taken there was an open tin box containing about five pounds in silver. Petty cash. He didn't touch that, neither did he touch the manager's expensive camera which was next to the petty cash box."

"The same story as the farm," Peter said. "Incidentally, I had a visit from the police yesterday."

"About the farm burglary?" Harvey looked somewhat dismayed.

"The constable didn't say as much, and I didn't ask, but that would be it. But they hadn't singled me out; they're calling on everyone who runs a car in the course of their work. They have Murchison's description and they know he was trying to cadge a lift."

"In this part of the world a stranger, especially a suspicious-looking one, couldn't expect to escape notice. What did you tell the police?"

"An ambiguous half-truth that seemed to satisfy. I didn't like doing it." Peter returned to the original subject. "He must have taken a risk coming right down almost into the centre of the town."

"Cross-country," Harvey said, "about five miles. More, if his hideout is tucked well up in the hills. But there wouldn't have been much danger involved. He has the Old People to look after him; he's provided with a sort of built-in radar."

He smiled a little at Peter's expression. "You'll get used to thinking in those sort of terms. And there's an odd sort of satisfaction in applying impossible fiction to real life."

"Satisfaction?" Peter wondered.

"Perhaps the wrong word. At least, in this context. My satisfaction comes from being able to remember the story and fit the parts of it into what is happening now. A selfish attitude when one considers the prospects. I must curb my enthusiasm. Incidentally, I've done the rounds of the local newsagents. Only one has records going back forty years. I became a collector of old American comics for the occasion, and the assistant went out of his way to help. He found an old price-list and then phoned the wholesalers. They came up with the information that our particular magazine had been published by a firm called Metz-Pudenski Publications with a Chicago address. But so far as they knew the firm is no longer in existence. They promised to make enquiries. It doesn't sound too hopeful, I'm afraid." Harvey pushed himself to his feet. "I'd better not keep you any longer."

Peter consulted his list. "I have a call on the Southam road. If you like, I can give you a lift as far as the bridge."

The other was grateful. "My bicycle still being at the farm, I had to walk to the main road and pick up the bus there. This way I'll be able to collect the bicycle again."

Peter nosed the car through the busy traffic in the square. His mind, yesterday numbed and unable to encompass events, had adjusted itself so that now he was able to think clearly again, to reason; with the feeling that he had stepped out of himself and was studying the thing with the dispassionate interest of a distant observer. Nature's compensating mechanism, he explained it to himself, having many times seen similar changes in mental outlook in patients suddenly told the necessity for undergoing major surgery. Once the initial shock of horrified incredulity had worn off, it was invariably followed by acceptance of the inevitable.

His passenger was silent until they reached the quieter stretch of road between the Colford New Estate and the tall wire fence of the Research Establishment. Then he leaned forward, patting his pocket.

"I forgot to tell you; I bought a one inch to the mile Ordnance Survey map of the district. Most of the caves are unexplored, but their entrances will be marked. We may find it useful."

Harvey glanced sideways. "Something else I forgot to tell you. I had to explain to Rosemary what has been going on. I happened to spot Edward setting out for a walk. He was heading towards the hills so I thought it wise to intercept. Rosemary came out while I was turning him round. So—" He shrugged. "I felt she would have to know sooner or later."

"How did she take it?" Peter asked anxiously.

"Hard to tell. Her reactions were much the same as yours. I don't think she believed me. She still has her flat in Colford. When I suggested she and Edward go there for a time, she said she'd think about it. When I pressed her she wanted to know how she could explain such a move to her mother when she comes out of hospital, there no longer being the excuse of the poltergeist for leaving the cottage."

Peter braked as the fork came in sight. "Her mother is another complication," he said, bringing the car to a halt.

Harvey sat for a while, hands resting on knees, not making any move to leave.

"I've considered advertising in the personal column," he observed inconsequently. "There are those people who can't bring themselves to throw anything away. . . . There's always a chance someone may have copies of that magazine stored away in a loft. But after forty years. . . ." He sighed, shaking his head.

A thought suddenly occurred to Peter and he voiced it without giving himself time to think.

"Garvey read the story. Is it likely he'll be able to remember anything about it?"

"You're forgetting, which is understandable, that Edward has lost his subconscious. And memory is the outward manifestation of the subconscious mind. The filing cabinet is empty. He is starting to fill it again."

Harvey looked thoughtful.

"Or is it as simple as that? Have all the file cards been transferred to the filing cabinet in Argred's mind? Certainly, Edward has lost his memory, but he still has a kind of instinct. He is able to recognise and put names to the things about him. He knows who he is and where he is. His limp is not nearly so pronounced, and he doesn't seem to be having as much trouble with the arthritis in his hands as he used to. Has pain gone with his subconscious? That's a thought. . . . And can one separate memory from instinct?" He opened the door without waiting for a reply. "Will you be paying us a visit later today?"

"Practice permitting," Peter said.

"Life must go on," Harvey said glibly. "I would like you to talk to Rosemary. I think she'll listen to you." He stepped into the road, slamming the door behind him.

Peter watched him walk towards the bridge, a stumpy, silver-haired figure with an almost military gait. Reaching for the starter he let his gaze lift from the road, first to the roofs of the farm buildings, then to the sloping fields, finally to the encircling hills. He wondered what Argred, who had once been Murchison, was doing now.

The entrance to the cave was a narrow cleft in the rock, partially screened by tall bushes. The tunnel into which it gave access twisted and turned for some distance before widening abruptly into a cavern with a low roof, dry walls and an even, scree-covered floor. No light filtered in from the outside. When Argred the Freeman had first found it, it had been in total darkness. Now it blazed with blue light. Cables snaked from a series of batteries set on the natural shelf of a rock ledge, connected with naked filaments suspended from the roof. Another ledge, wider and lower, served as a bench. Argred worked there, fierce white light darting and spluttering from the pieces of incomprehensible equipment his unconscious hands were assembling.

He had discovered that his hands worked of their own volition. They moved in obedience to the silent voices. The things they made were mysteries beyond his understanding. Yet at the same time there was an instinctive knowledge of the purpose they were to serve. At the beginning, working in darkness, he had known the things he was attaching to the roof were intended to make light. He knew that the tracery of silver wires that framed the outer entrance formed some kind of protective shield. He knew that the row of boxes about his head contained stored power. He knew that when his hands had finished assembling this new mystery it would have to be taken outside, to the stream, and placed in the water in a certain way and at a certain place, and that a cable from it would bring a new and even more potent power into the cave.

And this was only the beginning, the voices had told him. There was much to do yet, more tools to be searched for and found, so that the weapons could be constructed.

When darkness comes, whispered the voices while he worked, *you must go down into the plains again. . . .*

Peter drove out to Betley Hatch through an evening glory of cloudless skies, emerald fields and painted trees. The door of Harvey's cottage was closed and there was no sign of its occupant. Climbing from the car he walked towards the other cottage. The few moments while he waited for his knock to be answered he spent in wondering how Rosemary had taken Harvey's telling of the story. Then anxiety became concern, and concern suddenly changed to a fierce ecstasy of fear for her safety that startled him with its unexpected stabbing intensity. The door opened in the same moment that he realised the reason for the new emotion.

Rosemary wore a white dress with traceries of blue at collar and cuffs. Her small face bore the same look of strain it had carried the first time they had met.

She said: "Peter. . . ." And then, her eyes on his face, she came forward, into his arms, in the most natural way imaginable, as if it were something she had been doing all her life.

It was some time before she pushed herself gently away. The tension had smoothed away from her features, leaving in its place a kind of child-like tranquility. Like Peter, she seemed at a loss for something to say to break the little silence.

"I didn't expect that," she said finally.

"I think," he told her, "that it must have been coming on for some time. At least, so far as I'm concerned." He reached to smooth a strand of hair from her forehead. "It reached maturity as you opened the door."

"Just like that. . . ." Her answering smile teased. "You make me sound like an assurance policy." She opened the front room door.

"In here, Peter; Uncle Edward's in the kitchen. You haven't met him yet, have you?"

"Not yet." He chose the basket-chair he had used before. "Harvey tells me that he seems"—on the point of saying "changed" he substituted—"much better in himself."

"I've never known him so well, Peter. . . ." But she sounded doubtful. "His memory doesn't seem so good." She went on with a rush: "But that's not important, not when he seems so contented and settled. That's why I—"

"Why you don't want to take him away from here," he supplied.

She nodded. "I don't think I could bear it if he was to go back to being like he was before. Not after the way he's changed. . . . Harvey says we ought to leave the cottage."

"I know."

"All the things he told me." She gestured her helplessness. "The young man he took in. The story that Uncle Edward is supposed to have read. The things he says are happening now. But it's all impossible. It couldn't happen. It is impossible, isn't it, Peter?"

He had known that question would come. He had been wondering how best to answer it. Evasion would serve no useful purpose, and Harvey, who didn't seem to believe in half measures, would have told her everything, sparing her no part of it.

"They're impossible, Rosemary," he said quietly; "but they're happening. I'm afraid we've got to accept that."

"I think I knew what you would say." She moved restlessly to the window. "Harvey would never tell me anything so fantastic as that unless he was sure of himself. He can't bear being laughed at—I found that out a long time ago. But this. . . . I've been churning it over in my mind all day. It's like a nightmare; I feel I'm going to wake up any moment. I'm still not sure now whether I really believe it all. Harvey said I may be in danger. Peter, do you think we ought to leave here?"

And he had been waiting for that question as well.

But he hadn't been prepared for the way she was putting herself in his hands. Her voice and eyes told him she would do as he said. His previously partly-professional concern for her having been replaced by something very different, it was a responsibility he was more than happy to accept.

"Harvey says he doesn't think it would upset Uncle Edward now if we were to move," she said, watching his face. "But I don't know. . . . He's doing his best to help, but he's not a doctor."

Peter said: "All I know about your uncle is what I've heard. Uncle Andrew told me that in his opinion a move might aggravate his condition. I know there has been a change for the better, but in medicine, miracles, when they happen, don't happen overnight. We must still think of your uncle as having a deranged mind. It might not take very much to push him over the verge. I'm sorry to sound so brutal, Rosemary, but we can't afford to mince matters."

"I understand," she said quietly. "I'm more afraid for him than I am for myself. I think we ought to stay. For the time being, anyway; until something else happens. . . ."

"So far as we know," Peter said, "Argred—or Murchison; God knows which name we ought to call him—has collected a radio, a television set, some dry batteries and a collection of spare parts. I suppose they will be the 'tools' of the story. But I can't see him making any fearsome weapons out of those. I don't think there's any immediate danger."

Rosemary shivered. "I keep thinking about the man who wrote the story, Peter; imagining him sitting at a desk in a shabby little room, typing, inventing the characters in his head, making them do things—like puppets. . . . And now we're becoming part of it; we're part of the imagination of a man who wrote rubbish for children's comics." She laughed shakily. "I suppose it wouldn't have been so bad if it had been a good story. Harvey said it was rubbish."

"It's not quite like that," he told her, ignoring Harvey's talk of parallels. "We're not part of his imagination. We're only being affected by it. Although that's bad enough. There's no telling what his imagination cooked up."

He shook his head worriedly. "I don't like the idea of you staying out here. This is one of the times when I wish I wasn't a doctor, tied to a surgery and a bedside phone."

"Harvey's offered to move in with us, Peter."

"Then I should let him do that. He's an old man, but I'll be happier knowing he's with you."

"It'll be a squeeze." She took hold of his arm. "Now you'd better come and meet Uncle Edward."

But the kitchen was empty, the back door standing open.

"He's gone out again!" she exclaimed in dismay. "And I made him promise not to leave without first telling me."

Standing in the doorway she turned her concern on the hills.

"He was on his way up there this morning when Harvey stopped him and talked him out of it."

"How bad is his leg?" Peter asked her.

"It was very bad—until yesterday. It seems a lot better now. But he still limps a little."

"Then if he is trying to climb hills," he reassured her, "I don't think he'll get very far. And judging by the number of caves there are supposed to be up there, it's most unlikely he'll stumble upon Argred's particular one."

"Do you think—" she started, and then Harvey's soft, recognisable tattoo came to the front door.

"Edward?" He shook his head to her anxious enquiry. "No, I haven't seen him. How long has he been gone?"

"I'm not sure. Perhaps half an hour."

"Damn. . . ." Harvey looked at Peter and shrugged resignedly. "No use going after him; we don't even know if he's gone that way. . . ."

He couldn't remember coming this way before, along this steeply-climbing tortuous path, but still it seemed familiar. There was an odd feeling of having been here before—quite recently—so that at each blind corner, where the slopes shouldered the path aside, he almost seemed to know what view the next turn of the path would reveal.

Edward Garvey stopped, struggling for breath, one hand pressed against his side, when he reached the comparatively level ground of a narrow terrace fronting a scooped-out hollow. This place was familiar too; so much so that he stepped into purple shadow, looking about him, puzzling.

After a while he moved back into the waning sunlight. The same strange compulsion that had made him break his promise to Rosemary, that had brought him from the cottage and up into the hills, urged him to climb still further. He limped slowly along the path —now little more than a sheep-run—stopping from time to time to ease the growing pain in his leg.

There was a stream that had to be waded, the cream-frothing water reaching to the tops of his boots. A little further on there was another, this one wider and deeper, but with a flat-topped boulder that could be used as a stepping-stone. And it seemed to him that at some time, not all that long ago, he had had to cross both streams before, for he had known, even before coming upon them, that they would be there. And the entrances to the many caves he passed; those too he knew he had seen before, even seemed to recall exploring some of them.

There was a place where the path swung inwards and suddenly upwards, climbing sharply, so that after a few scrabbling steps, with fingers reaching futilely for a hand-hold, he had to give up the attempt, sliding back in a small avalanche of loose rubble. For a moment, with the breath tearing in his throat, his vision became clouded with a red mist. The mist cleared and by stepping away from the path a little, as far as he could go without risking a fall down the steep slope below, he was able to see past a rocky spur to where the path reappeared, dropping down again after its climb over the impassable crest, snaking distantly towards yet another stream.

Slanting sunlight danced on the water where it cascaded, a toy waterfall, into a miniature ravine. And in the pool below, thrusting out of the foaming water, was something—some arrangement of metal pieces, it seemed—that caught the fading light and tossed it back in glittering flashes of blue and silver. He narrowed wondering eyes, but the thing was too far away to be seen clearly. Beyond climbing the path, and now, with his leg, that was impossible, there was no way of getting closer to it. Edward Garvey stared at it while compulsion fought and lost the fight against utter weariness and pain. He turned to make his way slowly back the way he had come.

It was dusk when he reached the open ground that sloped down towards the rear of the cottage. The back door was closed but not locked. Limping along the passage, feeling his way in the darkness, ignoring the sound of voices in the front room, he went up the stairs and into his room, there to fling himself, just as he was, across the bed, immediately falling asleep.

The only sound to break the silence of the cave was the hiss and splutter of the soldering iron. When Argred laid it aside the silence was complete. As yet he didn't know the purpose of the thing his fingers had been constructing. It was an affair of thin, interlocking metal plates joined together with curiously-shaped rods, short lengths of cable trailing from each corner. He stepped away from the bench, flexing tired fingers, looking at them with momentary perplexity, waiting for the voices to issue their next command. But they didn't speak. Instead, his ears caught another sound, a distant one, as if an incautious foot had trod and slid on loose shale.

He moved swiftly, silently along the tunnel, listening as he went, not stepping out into sunlight when he reached the entrance, but standing with his back against the wall while he peered carefully out, meeting the force of the setting sun.

At first there was nothing to see, so that, his gaze raking the slopes, he put the sound down to a natural fall of rock. Then something moved, and a needle of rock became the silhouette of a man, turning, moving away, finally disappearing.

Argred waited a while before turning to re-enter the cave. As he took his hand from the wall the light fell across it. He raised it, puzzled again by its appearance, staring at it then lifting the other hand while he inspected both. Then he reached up to touch his face.

Horror was a cold emptiness, expanding inside him.

"My hands!" he shouted aloud. "My face! What is happening to me?"

And the voices were there, calm, soothing, reassuring.

Nothing is happening to you. Your face and hands seem strange to you because they belong to another man. Nothing is happening. . . .

The voices were never wrong. Argred went back along the tunnel.

But there was still something that wasn't as it should be. He tried to decipher the uneasiness. Then he knew what it was. An intruder had come close to the cave, and no warning had shrilled in his mind.

But that was impossible.

An intruder? The voices took up the puzzle, *No,* they said; *we would have known of the approach of a stranger.*

I saw him, thought Argred.

But they would have none of it. *A trick of light and shadow,* they told him. *Your eyes deceived you. Nothing alive has been near.*

The voices were never wrong.

Rosemary broke off what she was saying to listen.

"Was that the door of Uncle's room?"

"I'd better come with you," Peter said. Harvey followed them up the stairs. Fully dressed, Garvey lay fast asleep on top of the bed.

She exclaimed her relief. "Thank heavens! Is he all right, Peter?" She ended on a note of dismay. "His boots—on the clean bedspread."

She busied herself untying the laces while Peter gently took the thin wrist between his fingers.

"He seems all right; just exhausted." He turned the wrist over, opening the fingers, glancing up at Harvey. "Rock dust."

"His socks and feet are soaking," Rosemary discovered with more dismay.

"We'll just have to keep a sharper watch on him in future," Harvey said, and looked at his watch. "Time I was slipping over to my place to collect a few things for the kitchen armchair night ahead."

"Time I was on my way too," Peter said in the hall, and took Rosemary into his arms. Opening the front door, Harvey turned to watch the warmth of the farewell with a startled expression.

"I would appear to be losing my power of discernment," he observed when it was over. "How long, to use an over-worked expression, has this been going on?"

"Our mutual assurance policies matured earlier this evening," Rosemary informed him demurely.

"Assurance policies?" he echoed, and then seemed a little annoyed when Peter threw back his head to laugh. "An odd way," he said severely, "of describing an attachment."

The two men walked down the lane.

"Come inside for a few moments," Harvey invited when they reached his gate. "There are one or two things I want to show you."

His recently-purchased map was spread across the kitchen table, but first, before offering to explain the pencil marks on it, he switched on the small television set and stepped back, arms folded, watching the screen.

"I noticed it for the first time when I tried to get the six o'clock news," he said.

"You noticed what?"

The screen came to life.

"That," said Harvey, pointing unnecessarily with his chin.

The screen was blotted out by a shimmering mass of dancing lines. Vicious crackling drowned any other sound that might have been coming from the speaker.

"We never get interference out here," he said. "Friend Argred obviously has some kind of electrical equipment in operation. And suppressors apparently aren't part of the Old People's technology."

He switched off the set. "If this interference extends for any distance, then I suppose we'll have the post office out here. But they'll have trouble tracking it to its source."

Taking a pair of glasses from his pocket he set them on his face and moved to the table. Peter, who had never seen him wearing reading glasses before, was a little startled at the change in his features wrought by the heavy black rims. He bent obligingly over the map to study the sweeping half-circle traced by the stubby white fingers.

"The caves extend all along here," explained Harvey. "As you can see, the entrances have been indicated. Which doesn't help us very much. But there are a couple of points worth bearing in mind. No containers of any kind were taken at either of the two burglaries. With no means of storing water, Argred won't want to make a long journey every time he needs a drink. I feel he will have selected a cave with a stream close by.

"After the second burglary he must have had quite a heavy load to carry. That, I think, precludes any cave that has a very steep slope leading up to its entrance. I have marked three places which seem to fulfill these requirements."

"It sounds as if you've changed your mind about trying to find him," Peter said.

"Not really." The other straightened, removing his glasses and then pinching the bridge of his nose where they had rested. "I suppose it was more for something to do. . . . My suppositions may be completely wrong. I have another idea at the back of my mind. Edward. . . . Obviously he's been indulging in rough climbing, and wading through streams. Not, one would think, the kind of trip a man with his physical disabilities would choose for pleasure."

"I've been wondering about that myself."

"Yes." Harvey, going off at a tangent, went over to the sideboard to take something from one of the drawers. He laid it on the map.

"I only remembered this this morning. Took me quite a while to find it. Do you know how to use a gun?"

"I've never even handled one," Peter said.

"A Luger; a vicious-looking weapon." Harvey smiled. "Not the kind of thing one would expect to find in the possession of a retired schoolmaster. My only brother was killed in the war. This, and some photographs, are all I have left of him. I suppose I should have handed it in. But you know how it is. . . . I spent some time in cleaning it and getting its feel. It contains six bullets."

"Have you anything special in mind?" Peter asked steadily.

"Defensive purposes. It will be included with the rest of my impedimenta when I move over to Rosemary's place for the night. Shaving tackle, tooth-brush and automatic. I shall feel happier in my mind knowing it is close at hand."

They went to the front door.

"Are you going to put your uncle in the picture?" asked Harvey.

"I haven't made up my mind."

"Tell him. I don't think you'll have much trouble convincing him. We need all the help we can get."

Betley farm, a shadowy cluster of buildings, slept under the slow ebb and flow of the moontide.

Mr. Crabley opened his eyes, stared up at the ceiling and then sat upright against the pillows, listening, looking now at the pale oblong of the window. His groping fingers found the torch on the bedside table and switched it on. The alarm clock told him it was quarter past one.

At his side, his wife woke, asking sleepily: "What is it, Joe?"

"Something woke me; could've been Sheila barking. . . ." Then he was fully awake. "That bloke back again?"

He swung his legs out of bed, slid his feet into the waiting slippers, went across to the door and took down the coat that hung there, draping it roughly over his pyjamas.

"If it is," he promised grimly, "I'll give him something he won't forget in a hurry."

"Be careful, Joe," his wife said.

He grinned. "Don't you fret. I'm taking the gun."

Torch in hand he went down the stairs and into the kitchen. From a cupboard he took a double-barrelled shotgun and a handful of cartridges, ramming two into the breech and pouring the remainder into the coat pocket. Then he opened the back door and stepped out into the yard.

The night was silent and still. Moonlight pooled the cobbled yard. The gun held at waist-level, his eyes searching the surrounding darkness of out-buildings and trees, he padded quickly towards the barn.

At the door he shifted the gun to the crook of his arm while he raised the latch. The grating of metal didn't bring the expected response from the dog inside. Puzzled, Mr. Crabley found something more to perplex him. He lifted his face, turning it from side to side while he tried to trace and put a name to the unfamiliar smell that hung, sickly-sweet, on the still air. A smell, the alien strangeness of which set the thick flesh at the back of his neck creeping.

Almost angrily he threw the door open and called the dog's name. But there was no answering bark or scrabbling of paws. Then he switched on the torch. Its light ringed the dog, lying on the floor, muzzle froth-spattered, mouth gaping, eyes open and staring in the sightless glaze of death.

The clamour of the phone jerked Peter from heavy sleep. Eyes half-closed, not yet fully awake, habit made him turn on the light, consult the time—it was half past three—and then reach for the phone to utter the usual formula.

The man's voice at the other end, deep and gravelly, was curt to the point of sharpness.

"This is the Electronics Research Establishment. There has been an accident. Will you come as quickly as possible."

The last vestiges of sleep wiped away, Peter struggled up against the pillows. The voice cut into his request for further information.

"Use the main entrance. Carry some form of personal identification. Ask for Department Six. The guard will be expecting you." There was the click of the replaced receiver.

13

A strange aura of unreality hung over the early-morning streets. There was no traffic, the pavements were deserted, every window was dark and the street-lamps had been switched off. There was an emptiness as if life itself had ground to a halt.

Peter, accustomed to night-driving, but through town streets where life might slow its pace but never fade into nothing, found something bordering on the eerie in his drive out to the Establishment. It was a sensation heightened by apprehension of what he might find when he reached his destination.

He hadn't been too surprised to hear there had been trouble at a place where electronic equipment was made. It was almost an expected development. The voice on the phone had used the word "accident", but that could mean anything. The coincidence was too large to be swallowed. He felt sure that the person responsible for the first two burglaries had now decided to go to the electronic fountain-head. It was a more than disturbing thought.

The wire boundary fence loomed up in his headlights. He slowed, swinging from tarmac to gravel, stopping with the bonnet almost touching the metal gates. The car was immediately flooded with light. He wound down the window and a face filled the aperture.

"Dr. Hill," he said, fumbling for his wallet. "They are expecting me." A hand was waiting to take his driving licence. It was scrutinised and returned. But the peak-capped guard voiced doubt.

"They said an elderly man, Doctor."

"My uncle. We are in practice together. He is in hospital."

"I see." A circle of paper was deftly affixed to the windscreen. Peter reached for the brake as the gates swung open. "I was told to ask for Department Six."

"Straight ahead, sir," said the guard, touching his cap.

He drove along a wide drive with dimly-seen groups of flat-roofed buildings on either side. Another set of gates barred his way. A light blazed. A shadow inspected the paper on the windscreen.

"First turning on the left," a voice told him. "You will find someone waiting." Gravel grated as the gates opened.

A longer drive this time. More buildings looming up and a figure stepping out in front to flag him down. Case in hand, Peter followed a dark-uniformed guard up a concrete path and in through an anonymous door. A brightly-lit corridor with echoing walls ended at another door. His escort ushered him silently inside.

The man who came to his feet behind a desk had a square face and unsmiling grey eyes. Rimless spectacles allied with close-cropped grey hair to further the impression of dispassionate efficiency.

"Dawson," he introduced himself curtly; "in charge of security. I understand you have come in place of your uncle who is in hospital. We are checking now."

Peter looked from the rimless spectacles to the other occupant of the room, the lanky man with thin fair hair who stood at the side of the desk.

"I gathered there was some urgency," he said.

"All in good time," Dawson said coldly. "Security is more important than urgency."

The phone buzzed softly and the fair-haired man reached out a long arm to pick up the receiver.

"Yoxall." He listened, replaced the receiver and nodded at Dawson. "It's all right."

"You can see your patient now, Doctor," Dawson said, and moved to open the door. Peter followed him back along the passage, past the entrance to another door. Inside the small room yet another uniformed guard stood at the side of the stretcher laid on the floor. Peter stooped over its occupant. Blood covered the side of Mr.

126

Brownlee's face and had trickled down to stain his shirt and the canvas of the stretcher. His eyes were closed and he was breathing heavily through his open mouth. Peter probed carefully at the matted hair, touched the exposed wound, then felt for the pulse with one hand while with the other he lifted one of the closed eyelids. Then he looked up into the expressionless faces of his small audience.

"How did it happen?"

"We don't know yet," Dawson said blandly.

"How long ago?"

"Neither do we know that yet. He was found, in this condition, about ten minutes before you were called."

"Has he regained consciousness at all?"

"No," Dawson said impatiently. "One of my men found him in the compound, called for assistance and stayed by his side until the stretcher had been brought. I had him carried in here—the first-aid room."

"He shouldn't have been moved," Peter said brusquely.

"It was essential," rejoined the other with matching curtness.

Peter straightened. "The bleeding has stopped, but the wound requires stitching. He may be suffering from mild concussion. He should be taken to hospital."

"No," Dawson stated in a voice that brooked no argument. "That is out of the question. He must be treated here. I have my reasons."

"If I had been given more details over the phone," Peter said acidly, bristling at the overbearing attitude, "I could have brought the necessary things with me. If you refuse to have him sent to hospital then I must insist he be taken to my surgery."

Dawson stroked his chin at the ultimatum. "The stretcher will fit into the back of one of our small vans," he said finally.

"He'll be all right propped up in the back of my car."

"You're the doctor." Dawson, patently unhappy about the arrangement, turned a flinty gaze on his colleague. "This had better be your pigeon, Yoxall."

The other wasted no time. Two guards were called and detailed to carry the stretcher and its burden out to the car. Peter superintended the lifting of Brownlee to the back seat. He wasn't very surprised when Yoxall folded his lanky length alongside the still unconscious Brownlee. Security, it seemed, had no intention of letting the injured man out of its sight. Both sets of gates were open ready for the car's passage.

"A nasty accident," Peter observed conversationally as the car swung into the main road.

"Yes," agreed Yoxall.

"Do you get many accidents like that?"

"No," said Yoxall.

Peter made no further attempt to open a conversation with his uncommunicative passenger. It was Yoxall who finally broke the silence as the car drew up outside the surgery, asking tersely: "Anyone else in?"

"Housekeeper," Peter retorted with equal brevity, and, anticipating the next question: "Her room's at the top of the house. We shouldn't disturb her."

They carried the unconscious man up the steps and into the surgery, Peter using his elbow to indicate the leather-covered couch. "On there."

Stripping off his coat and jacket he trundled the metal trolley to the side of the couch and laid out an array of instruments on its glass top. Yoxall eyed the preparations with a certain look of apprehension. At the sink, Peter rolled up his shirt sleeves and made an over-elaborate job of scrubbing his hands.

"It'll be rather a messy job," he remarked pleasantly. "I much prefer working without an audience. That's if it's all the same to you."

It was. The other moved with alacrity and undisguised relief to the door. "I'll wait outside. Let me know as soon as you've finished, or if he comes round."

Peter dried his hands, filled a bowl with water and took it to the trolley, removing most of the unnecessary instruments.

"All right," he said. "You can wake up now."

Mr. Brownlee opened his eyes and grinned weakly. "I thought I 'ad you fooled as well, Doc."

"Give me credit for knowing when a patient's playing possum."

"Is it bad?"

"Not as bad as you would have had us all believe." Peter swabbed gently with water-soaked wool. "But it will need a couple of stitches. I gather by this charade that you didn't take my advice about not poking your nose into things that aren't your concern?"

"Somethin' like that. 'ell. . . ." The patient flinched.

"Save your energies." Peter dropped the stained swab into the bowl. "The worst is to come. So what happened?"

"You wouldn't believe me if I told you," said Brownlee with unusual earnestness. "You'd say I was off my nut. That's why I played it like I did, to give me time to think up some sort of yarn they'll believe. If I told 'em what really 'appened they'd put me away."

"Try it out on me," Peter said, using forceps to pick up the ready-threaded curved needle from the bowl of antiseptic.

"Now? With me like this? I can't even think straight, Doc. I don't even—" He flinched again, this time at the first prick of the needle.

"It'll help if you talk," Peter said. "This doesn't warrant local anaesthetic."

"I know what you mean." The patient managed a sickly grin. "Take my mind off it. You didn't split on me last night. . . . Well, I was where I wasn't supposed to be, playin' poker in the 'ut with Clinton an' Torry, the two off-duty guards. At two sharp, Howarth —one of the old guards—comes off an' Clinton goes to take over. Howarth pops along to the canteen an' we wait for the other guard, Southern, to show up for Torry to replace 'im—"

"Steady," Peter warned. "This may hurt."

"Ar—" Brownlee grunted feelingly. "You weren't kiddin'. Well, at 'alf past two Torry goes to see what's keepin' Southern, leavin' me on my tod. After ten minutes or so I get sort of jumpy an' I go out to see for myself what's goin' on." He paused.

"Keep talking," Peter said. He had completed the minor operation and was now deliberately wasting time. He looked at the door behind which Yoxall was presumably kicking his impatient heels. From past experience he knew that voices in the surgery couldn't be heard in the hall.

"Moonlight," said Brownlee; "almost as bright as day. Enough for me to make out the perimeter wire. And right away I spots that something's wrong. There's a 'ole in the wire, only I can't see it all that clear because of a kind of blueish 'aze. An' there's somethin' else wrong. They 'ave a current runnin' through the fence, so that if anyone tampers with it, even touches it, the alarm sets up. Well, there's this ruddy great 'ole, an' the bells aren't ringin' an' the lights 'aven't come on. Which don't make sense, an' if I was to tell them, they wouldn't believe me.

"I make towards the 'ole, an' it's then I notice the smell. Wicked, it were—" He shuddered graphically. "Never smelt anythin' like it before, an' don't want to again. Still in me nose. . . . I looks round, tryin' to figure out where it's comin' from, an' then I sees that the door of the big lab is wide open when by rights it should be shut an' double-locked. I goes inside. There's enough moonlight for me to make out Torry lyin', spark out, on the floor; an' behind 'im, Southern, sitting propped against a bench with 'is eyes closed too."

"They didn't tell me anyone else had been injured," Peter inserted.

"They're all right." Brownlee turned on his grin for a moment. "I 'eard Dawson and Yoxall talkin' while I was supposed to be unconscious. The guards 'ad both come round but they didn't know what 'ad 'appened. They'd seen the door open, gone inside an' then just flaked out."

"But you went in, and you didn't flake out."

"Maybe because I weren't in long enough. I turned to leg it back to the 'ut to phone for 'elp. An' then I slowed down, trying to figure out what sort of yarn I could spin for bein' where I wasn't supposed to be. I look back, an' there's this thing—a man, it could've been —comin' out of the lab. I can't see it clearly because there's the same sort of 'aze as there was at the fence. He's tall an' thin, 'is face is just a blur, 'e walks like 'is legs are on hinges an' there's some sort of contraption fastened on 'is chest. I never seen anythin' like it before. I was damned scared, I don't mind admittin'. It were like somethin' from another world; like those things you see in some of the films. . . ."

Or like something from a children's science-fiction comic, Peter thought.

"I turned an' ran," Mr. Brownlee said simply. "An' I ran smack into one of the lamp standards, an' that's the last thing I know."

Peter put a dressing on the stitched wound and fixed it in place with strips of plaster. "And that's you fixed up like new."

"What the 'ell am I goin' to tell 'em?" the patient asked, raising himself on one elbow. "I can't tell 'em what really 'appened."

"You know better than me what kind of people they are," Peter said. "It always pays to tell the truth. If they don't believe you, then that's their affair."

"An' if I gets the push an' gets put away into the bargain," supplied Mr. Brownlee bleakly, "then that's mine."

"I have the feeling that at the moment—" Peter broke off, finding he had little in the way of comfort or advice to offer. "You'll have to wriggle out of it the best you can, I'm afraid. We can't keep your escort waiting any longer." He opened the door. "All through," he informed Yoxall.

"He's come round," Yoxall said accusingly.

"I didn't think it advisable to interrupt the operation to break the news to you."

"Has he said anything?"

"I think you'll find he's in no fit state to do much talking," Peter said.

Without asking permission, Yoxall picked up the phone and set the dial whirling.

"Yoxall. I'm speaking from Dr. Hill's surgery. Get a car out here to pick me up."

He slammed the receiver back. "Under the circumstances I think it would be as well if you were to come with us, Doctor. I have the feeling Mr. Dawson will want to talk to you."

Peter returned from putting the instruments away. "I have a practice to look after. I've already lost the best part of a night's sleep." He nodded towards the couch. "And my patient ought to be taken home and put to bed."

"We have a sick bay at the Establishment," said Mr. Yoxall.

"He's in no condition to be subjected to an interrogation, if that's what you have in mind."

"I'm afraid you must leave others to be the judge of that now, Doctor. Is he able to walk?"

Mr. Brownlee joined in the conversation for the first time. He swung his legs to the ground. "I'll manage," said he.

Some ten minutes later Yoxall had the last word. With the sound of a car drawing up outside he took Brownlee's arm in a firm grip.

"We will probably want to talk to you tomorrow, Doctor," he warned with heavy significance.

It seemed that the security arrangements at the Research Establishment were as efficient as Peter had privately given them credit for. No word of the night's events had leaked out, or if it had, it hadn't leaked as far as Mrs. Charnley. Her only comments as she laid the breakfast table were the usual ones about the weather.

After lunch he drove to the hospital. On the terrace Dr. Hill enjoyed the sunshine, reclining at ease in a chair, hands clasped over his comfortable rotundity, legs hoisted to the balustrade.

"The lap of luxury," Peter said.

His uncle opened one lazy eye. "Making the most of the placid existence while I can. And how are things in the outside world? From news that drifts in I gather they're not all that placid."

"They're not," Peter told him.

"A rash of burglaries. It's years since Colford's seen anything like that." Dr. Hill opened the other eye and brought his brow down to meet it. "And from your expression I would say there's something more."

Peter borrowed an expression of Brownlee's. "You're not kidding." He took out his cigarettes. There were no short cuts. He would have to go back to the start and plough through the whole thing.

The new things, the strange objects that he had brought back from the building in the wire enclosure, were laid out on the floor of the cave. The voices were silent, as if they too were studying these metal and wire shapes. Argred the Freeman waited patiently for the voices to return, for his hands to resume their labours.

There were scraps of food on one of the rock shelves, the remains of his last meal. It had been a day and a night since he had last eaten, but for some reason he was neither hungry nor thirsty. It had been longer than that since he had last closed his eyes in sleep, but there was no weariness in his body.

Eating, drinking and sleeping were the weaknesses of ordinary men. He was no ordinary man now. His new body was filled with the strength and wisdom of the Old People. There was no tiredness, no pain; perhaps—even no death. He was a superior being to the futile people of the plains. Destroying them, when the voices said the time was ripe, would be as easy as setting his foot on a teeming ant-hill. As easily as he had destroyed the strange animal that had tried to give warning of his presence; as easily as he had disposed of the two men who had tried to bar his way. He could have killed them too, would have done, but for the voices warning: *No; not yet. We are not ready yet.* . . .

But the weapons would soon be ready. Soon the voices would speak again, taking control of his fingers. He lifted his hands in the harsh glare of the naked filaments, looking at them disinterestedly, seeing where patches of the new, brown scaliness were growing and spreading between high-ridged bone. The Old People knew of the change that was taking place in his flesh, were responsible for it, and so there was no cause for concern. The same change was happening to the rest of his body. He had already discarded the leather foot-coverings, finding it impossible to walk in them. Now he stripped off the soft leather jacket and the thinner fabric covering beneath, throwing them aside, exposing the withering parchment of the rib-cage and the flattened, sunken stomach.

The drying flesh was pock-marked with the same shell-hard discolouration. And his face? There was no polished surface, no pool of still water that might hold his reflection. He had to rely upon touch, and there was little feeling left in his fingers. They gripped the tools with no sensation of touch. They felt the lines of his jaw now, sensing shape without texture. They found the new hollows of sunken cheeks, moved to the ridged forehead, touched the line between flesh and hair. And when they came down again there were matted tresses of tawny hair caught in the horned nails. He let the dull mass of hair fall to the ground.

And then something came into his mind—a vague, dimly-seen picture of a strange place with a circle of watching, strange faces.

And hair, locks of coal-black hair, falling to a white sheet. When he closed his eyes, wondering at the picture, willing it to come clearer, the voices suddenly clamoured, commanding him to return to work.

And when he opened his eyes again, looking about him, he saw that he had been making his way, without knowing what he was doing, along the tunnel, towards the sunlight.

Dr. Hill swung his feet to the stone flags of the terrace and was silent for a while, face hidden while he brooded over the garden. Peter took out his cigarette case to discover he had emptied it during the telling of the story.

"You should have told me when it first started," observed his uncle mildly.

Peter returned the case to his pocket. "I was in two minds. Harvey wanted me to. But at the start—"

"I'd have listened to you. Even if it did seem to be just another of Harvey's theories. But the body was real enough. . . ." Dr. Hill shook his head. "You should have done something about that."

"I only had Harvey's word that Murchison was dead," Peter said. "If I had seen the body for myself, it would have been different. I had to go by common sense."

"I suppose I would have done the same." Hands deep in the pockets of his dressing-gown, Dr. Hill launched into quiet savagery. "What a damned, unholy mess! Where are we—back in the Dark Ages, wallowing in witchcraft and demoniacal possession? Or reaching into a future where the psychiatric answer to schizophrenia could be the complete removal of one of the conflicting personalities?"

"Perhaps a little of each," Peter said.

"Edward Garvey is the keystone. What do you make of him?"

"I've only seen him the once—close to, that is—and then he was asleep. Don't forget I have a practice to look after. I can't be in two places at the same time."

"We appear to have a surfeit of that sort of thing already," said Dr. Hill with grim humour, and came to his feet to go into the ward, stubbing at the bell-push before opening the narrow cupboard by the bed.

"One thing about a private ward," he said, tossing clothing on the bed, "is that one's personal belongings aren't carried away to some remote store." He took off his dressing-gown. The nurse came in as he was unbuttoning the pyjama jacket.

"I'm discharging myself," he informed her crisply. "I know what I'm doing, and I know the drill. Tell Sister I'll drop a note to the Registrar."

She retired hastily, protest on her face but unvoiced, when he reached for the cord of his trousers. Peter turned to watch the garden during the few minutes it took his uncle to dress.

"I gather from your silence you expected me to do this," said Dr. Hill as they walked along the corridor.

"I did," Peter said. "And I've known you long enough not to waste my breath arguing."

"Which is probably why you left it as long as possible before telling me the story. What have you got on the agenda for this afternoon so far as the practice is concerned?"

"I'm not sure. Eight or nine calls, I think."

"It's four o'clock now. You're going to be kept busy till evening surgery."

They emerged into the afternoon sunshine.

"The Establishment," said Dr. Hill as they made their way towards the car. "I'll make that my first port of call; unofficially to see what I can find out about last night's episode, officially to take over our patient. What was his name again?"

"Brownlee."

"A new name to me. But that's a detail. Dawson's my man; we're old friends. Yoxall—I've not had much to do with him. I believe he's a kind of liaison officer between local security and London."

"From what I saw of them," Peter observed, "I can't see you getting much out of either of them."

"You never can tell." Dr. Hill smiled. "Don't underestimate my powers of unobtrusive persuasion. Drop me off at the main entrance. When I've examined our patient—that's if he's still there—I'll pick up a bus to the bridge and walk the rest of the way to Betley. I'll expect you out there as soon as you've finished surgery."

14

There were no visible signs of unusual activity at the Research Establishment. Peter watched his uncle cross the road towards the forbidding metal gate. A guard came to meet him, hand lifted to peaked cap in a salute of recognition. The gate was opened to allow him inside. He walked slowly along the gravelled drive so that the accompanying guard had to adjust his pace.

Peter frowned at the adjustment. He remembered his uncle as having an almost athletic stride. He didn't know just how bad the heart-attack had been—Uncle Andrew had been evasive—but even a mild attack, which was how Sister had described it, could leave its mark on someone who wouldn't see sixty again. He would have to keep a careful eye on the old man.

He consulted the list pinned to the dashboard. Eight names, three new to him which meant visits would be necessary. Of the remainder, four were those of regulars, patients of long-standing to whom a day's delay would make little difference. Mentally crossing them off his list, he checked the time. With luck he should be able to get through the others in time to give Uncle Andrew a lift to Betley.

The first three calls were soon disposed of. But the last, some distance along the Southam road, took difficulty in finding and the visit itself took longer than he had bargained for. It was past five when he drove over the bridge. He met up with his uncle on the doorstep of Rosemary's cottage.

"I cut the list," he explained to the other's elaborate gesture of consulting his watch, "in the hope of being in time to give you a lift."

"Unprofessional," remarked Dr. Hill, "but showing consideration." And as the door opened: "Rosemary. . . . And how have you been standing up to all this excitement?"

Peter was content to remain in the background, but Rosemary smiled at him over his uncle's shoulder and drew him into the conversation. "Two doctors at the same time. . . ."

"Almost a medical convention," said Dr. Hill.

She stepped invitingly aside. "You'll find Harvey in the kitchen, Doctor."

In the hall, Peter set his hands on her shoulders and gazed searchingly into her face.

"So nothing else has happened," he discovered with relief.

She laughed. "Can you tell that just by looking at me?"

"I can read you like a book." He drew her towards him.

"Uncle Edward tried to go out again this morning," she informed him after a while, her voice a little muffled by reason of her face being pressed against his breast. "He was making towards the hills. Harvey had to stop him again. And I went to visit Mother this afternoon. She'll be coming home early next week."

"That's good to hear," he said slowly.

She sighed. "I know. . . . But perhaps things will have sorted themselves out by then." She paused. "On the way back, in the bus, everything seemed so normal. Women with shopping-baskets; children . . . laughing and talking. It seemed impossible that anything could be wrong. I tried to tell myself that everything was all right, that the police are bound to search the hills, and then they'll find him and take him away and everything will be over."

"It could work out that way," he replied, trying to make his voice convincing.

"So when I got back again I started trying to make the place look like it used to. At least, it was something to do." Disengaging herself from his arms she opened the parlour door. "I went through Mother's things upstairs, trying to find ornaments and pictures to fill the spaces."

137

The previously obvious gaps had been filled. Framed photographs had been set in a row along the top of the old-fashioned piano. The one in the centre drew Peter's attention. It was the head and shoulders of a young man with a narrow face, indefinite features and a shock of very black hair.

"Uncle Edward," said Rosemary. "But it must have been taken a long time ago. I can't remember him like that."

"He's changed," Peter said inadequately.

"The way I like to remember him is when Mother used to take me to see him in his lodgings. I suppose I'd be ten or eleven. . . . He just used to sit there, smiling, not speaking. I didn't know about his trouble then. He just seemed an ordinary nice sort of person."

"You think a great deal of him."

She went to stand by the window, fingering the loops of blue ribbon that held the curtains in place. "He's never harmed anyone. He's never been trouble to anyone but himself. Harvey once said that we all have two sides to us, and the good and bad is all mixed up together so that even a really good person always has a little bad in him. But with Uncle Edward, the two separated completely, and it was the pushing away of the bad into the back of his mind that made him the way he is. But that didn't seem right to me; it meant that only someone who wasn't quite right in the mind could be wholly good."

"That's a subject even the experts are divided about," Peter said slowly. "And Harvey's no expert. I suspect in his own way he was trying to make you feel better. But you know what they say about good intentions. I like Harvey, and respect him; but he's an old man who's spent nearly all his life in a class-room environment. I can't help feeling that in a queer sort of way he's almost enjoying what is happening. I think he feels he's doing something useful again. Perhaps I'm doing him an injustice."

"Perhaps." Rosemary changed the subject. "It was good to see your uncle again, Peter. I didn't know he was ready to leave hospital."

"He wasn't. He discharged himself."

She was startled. "He shouldn't have done that. I thought he didn't look his usual self."

"He's far from being his usual self." Peter shook his head unhappily. "I knew this would happen when I told him what had been going on. I put it off as long as possible, but after last night it seemed pointless to wait. I have the feeling that before very long it will be common knowledge that something out of the ordinary is happening."

"After last night, Peter?"

He explained briefly about his visit to the Establishment. Her first concern was for Mr. Brownlee.

"Was he badly hurt, Peter?"

"Not badly. I made more of the treatment than the injury called for just to give him time to tell me his version of events."

"And he actually saw him?"

"He saw someone or something. There wasn't time for me to ask questions; Yoxall was cooling his heels outside. But Uncle Andrew may have found out more. He's just come from the Establishment now."

They went to the kitchen where Harvey and Dr. Hill pored through the haze of Harvey's pipe over the map on the table.

"You've been a long time," observed Dr. Hill.

Harvey was archness itself. "I expected them to be much longer." His over-done significance caused the other to raise his usual eyebrow and remark generally: "I suspected as much," and to Rosemary in particular: "You'll find it no picnic being associated with a doctor."

"I've taken that into consideration," she assured him.

"Apart from anything else," he pointed out gravely, "they talk shop. To the uninitiated, a dinner accompanied by a commentary on a post-mortem can be disconcerting to say the least. An iron constitution is needed for that sort of thing. Which is one of the reasons why I've never wished myself upon some unsuspecting female."

Harvey decided the thing had gone far enough.

"We were discussing Crabley's dog," he told Peter. "It was killed last night, and the vet can't give the cause. It seems that Crabley heard a sound during the night, went out to investigate and found the body. He saw or heard nothing else, but he noticed a strange, unpleasant smell."

Dr. Hill took over. "Harvey suggests that Argred—as I suppose we must call him—wouldn't make a detour to dispose of a dog. Which could mean that the farm is on the direct line between the Establishment and the cave where he is hiding."

"Brownlee said he noticed an unpleasant smell too," Peter said.

"Brownlee. . . ." His uncle nodded. "He is doing very nicely. They haven't allowed him home yet. I gather he must have told them the same story that he told you. They don't believe him. For one thing, he couldn't have seen a hole in the fence. It's still intact. But the laboratory door was open, even though it was still locked. Which needs explaining. . . .

"Dawson's theory is that someone had duplicate keys made, unlocked both locks, opened the door and then, while it was still open, re-locked it before removing the keys. Dawson wanted to know if the bump on Brownlee's head could have caused him to have hallucinations. I said there was always that possibility." He paused. "Quite a lot of electronic equipment is missing. Dawson wouldn't say what."

Peter went to lean against the sink, his hands on the cool porcelain.

"I think I can hazard a guess as to one of the things they are working on there," he said. "I treated Brownlee earlier for a rather unusual burn that he'd got by prying."

"They are working on electron-beams," supplied Dr. Hill. "There's no great secret about that."

"I was thinking about a laser. But a laser with a refinement. Brownlee's burn was only superficial, but it became badly infected. I wondered if it was possible to transmit a virus along the beam of a laser."

"I've never heard of such a thing. I would think it to be impossible. But that's only a theory of yours, Peter, and we're having a surfeit of those. My ex-schoolmaster friend here has one to explain both the mystery of the hole in the fence that wasn't there, and the unlocked, locked door."

140

Harvey accepted the invitation, removing his glasses and laying them on the map.

"When looking for an explanation we cannot confine ourselves to practical things. We have to look through the eyes and mind of the writer of the story. Writing that story, it was within his power to invent any device he fancied. Whether or not those devices were impossible to our way of thinking makes no difference at all. He made them work on paper, so they will work now, in real life. We cannot be guided by reason.

"Let us suppose he came up with a device that could temporarily make metal permeable. That would explain the contraption attached to his chest, the gap in the fence and the door that was opened without first being unlocked. Argred must also carry some form of weapon. He used it to kill the dog and stun the two guards."

Harvey folded his arms and leaned back with an air of satisfaction.

Peter, finding nothing to say, was silent.

Dr. Hill cleared his throat. "Interesting," he allowed mildly. "But it doesn't get us anywhere." He laid his hand on the map. "Neither, I'm afraid, does this. We must consider facts, not theories. They will not call in the police to investigate the theft from the Establishment. It was clear from the way Dawson spoke he had already made up his mind it was an inside job. He will deal with it himself, and I'm certain he will not try to connect it with the previous two burglaries. There will be no scouring of the countryside in search of the culprit.

"So far so good. With all the evidence to support it, I have to accept the fact that Edward's mind has divided, and that part of it is now activating Murchison's body. I gather that as a result he has lost his memory, but still retains some form of instinct.

"Yesterday, despite attempts to dissuade him, he went climbing in the hills. He made another determined attempt this morning. This would seem to indicate some kind of compulsion, which in its turn points to the possibility of there still being a link between the two parts of his mind. I feel we should try to exploit that link."

"A suggestion I had been on the point of broaching myself," Harvey said smugly. "Sir Jeremy Miles-Ferguson—you will know the name—was a pupil in the actual class that used the story of Argred the Freeman in their lessons. He is the only former pupil of that particular class whose progress I have been able to follow. But one could hardly approach a titled Harley Street specialist to ask if he happens to know the ending of a story he read forty years ago in a comic. Unless one could offer a good excuse for such a request. And what better than the truth? And at the same time ask for his professional assistance as a psychiatrist?"

"I've heard of him," Dr. Hill said dryly. "And I can well imagine his reception of such a tale, even if it did come from one of his old schoolteachers. And even if he could bring himself to take it seriously —which I very much doubt—the mountain still wouldn't come to Mahomet. And we can't risk taking Mahomet to the mountain. No, what I have in mind is rather different. Unorthodox"—he threw a quick glance in Peter's direction—"but, under the circumstances, logical. I've been told what took place during Mrs. Cookson's second visit. Not only did her presence somehow trigger off events, but apparently she was also in touch with that part of Edward's mind that has since become Argred. She may be able to make contact again. It is possible she may be able to tell us where he is hiding and what his intentions are."

"You did warn it was unorthodox," Peter said.

"For some reason," observed Harvey, "Peter appears to have taken a dislike to Mrs. Cookson. Or perhaps it's her methods. But who can say just where to set the dividing line between psychiatry and the near-occult?"

"It seems to be our only course," Dr. Hill said equably. "This mental link is the only positive thing we have to go on. We could give Edward his head, of course; let him make for the hills and then follow in the hope he would lead us to Argred. But for obvious reasons that wouldn't be advisable. His physical condition is poor, his mental state worse. Any shock could do him untold harm."

He consulted his watch.

"Getting on for five-thirty," he informed Peter, coming stiffly to his feet. His face was grey-tinged and there were mosaics of fine lines at the corners of his eyes. "I'll pay Mrs. Cookson a visit while you're taking surgery."

He rested his hands on the table, his weight on his hands while he smiled at Rosemary. "I think it would be best if you could try to keep your uncle in his room. And try not to worry about all this. I'm sure it will sort itself out."

And to Harvey, having trouble folding the map into its original creases: "You'll be staying with her?"

"I've moved in for the duration," Harvey reported, and patted his pocket. "Armed to the teeth."

"Fine." Dr. Hill was a commander satisfied with the disposition of his forces. "We'll find our own way out." And an afterthought for Peter's benefit: "No time for protracted farewells."

He stumbled on the path outside, but shook Peter's gesture of help away, grunting testily: "I can manage."

In the car he leaned back, closing his eyes. "I would have taken a look at Edward," he said in a tired voice, "but Harvey said he was asleep."

"Do you have to trail out to Mrs. Cookson's place?" Peter asked, reaching for the starter. "Couldn't you ring her?"

"It's not the kind of thing you can discuss at length over a telephone," said Dr. Hill. "It'll have to be the whole thing; the telling will take some time."

For all he knew he was going to be late for evening surgery, Peter still drove slowly, braking carefully, taking the corners with elaborate care in an effort to make the journey as less tiresome as possible for his passenger. Guilt tinged his concern. He was the one responsible for Uncle Andrew being here, in this condition. Now he had the further complication of a sick man who needed watching over. It was only too obvious from the grey face at his side that even the few short hours out of hospital had taken their toll.

Edward Garvey was a neutral factor. That left four people who were the only ones who knew about the impossible thing that had happened and who could try to put an end to it before—Before what? That was something he didn't know, was almost afraid even to guess at. That was something only that writer of forty years ago knew.

Four people. . . . An old man, not yet recovered from one heart-attack, likely to have another at the first hint of excitement; an even older man who seemed to be taking an almost child-like delight in the situation; a girl, and himself. . . .

And what could four such futile people hope to do against something that could stun and kill, that could walk where it pleased, through metal fences and locked doors?

The miniature ravine was an unexpected deformity of the hills. It was as if, at the beginning of time, a gigantic hand had reached down from the skies, palm sideways, to slice through the smooth-moulded folds of green and brown, exposing the bleak harshness of grey granite sub-strata.

There was only the one way in. The path, such as it was, a barely perceptible thinning of wiry turf, clung to the slopes, twisting and turning with the contours, with the ravine and its waterscape of cascades, foaming stream and swirling pools in view for some time, from a distance, before a massive shoulder of rock thrust outwards, diverting it, forcing it to climb steeply, letting it drop again beyond the crest, to lose itself in the rock terraces of loose scree that fronted the curving rock-face and sloped down to the boulder-impeded stream at the bottom.

There was no pretence of humanity left now about the being that had once been Clive Murchison. The fabric that had once covered its legs had been torn into strips and used to bind roughly about the waist and thighs. It stood grotesquely in the foaming water of the stream, its distorted fingers fumbling clumsily at the metal and coiled-wire construction that stood out of the water like some nightmare piece of sculpture. The voices had commanded that adjustments be made, and so it had obeyed, leaving the cave, having to stoop now to pass through the entrance, lurching down the slope to the water. It felt neither the ice-bite of the stream nor the stab when a sharp edge of metal cut deeply into what had once been flesh.

For some time now there had been a difference to the voices. They were still there, clamouring their commands, but there were times when they became indistinct, less insistent, almost drowned by a strange new intrusion. Voices of another kind, and not only voices, but pictures; shadowy, formless shapes and fragments of scenes that built up into sudden completeness but were gone before there was time to study them, to wonder at their origin. Mind-pictures of people and places that were strange and bewildering, and yet, at the same time, hauntingly familiar.

The hands finished their work. The being rose to its height, awaiting the next orders. When they came it used a projection of rock to haul itself awkwardly to the bank. There was no difference between the warm air and the almost glacial water of the stream.

At the entrance to the cave it paused, the voices fading, yet another picture forming on the curtain of its mind. A road, a smooth-surfaced endless road; a hand outstretched, fingers curved against the palm, circle of metal poised on the thumb. Then the metal spinning into the air, glinting in the light, dropping, caught. . . . There was some meaning to be read from the strange engravings on the disc—a decision to be taken. The familiar and unfamiliar vehicle that came lumbering along the road towards him was connected with that decision.

The scene flickered out of existence.

Return to the workshop, commanded the voices.

Shards of pale colour dancing on grey mist became another scene. Now, the endless lines of gleaming machines, fading away into infinity, seen through the glazing eyes of a dying man. Marna was there, wrapped in her cloak. And Kolda the Stranger, arrogant, proud. . . .

Into the scene came the clamour of the silent voices, dispelling it, whirling the pieces away. But there was yet another waiting to take its place, another confusion of solidifying shapes. This time, a tiny room; a familiar bed; a window with soft curtains; sunlight warm and comforting. . . . And a feeling of security, of this being his place where no harm could come to him. A need to sleep, to be lost, to become part of the white blankets of oblivion.

And with this scene a feeling of compulsion, a sensation so compelling that it held the picture intact against the soft thunder of the intruding voices. The way out of the ravine was steep, the path of loose stones, on which dead feet slipped and stumbled. The room dissolved, vanished; but the compulsion remained.

Work, the voices shouted on the slippery turf track beyond the shoulder of rock.

Come back, they cried, fading now, at the place where a stream had to be forded.

They were silent, lost in distance, at the place where the path became a clear brown ribbon of trodden earth. There was silence now. Fragments of pictures appeared and melted. Faces impinged on faces. Consciousness fought with consciousness, but there was no mastery. Awareness had gone. The only reality was the driving compulsion.

Danger! A new voice whispered as the path emerged from a hollow into the open, with the valley suddenly spreading itself below.

Danger! Louder now, as the path rose between clumps of bracken and gorse, with the road coming into view.

Beyond the bushes a gentle slope of grass led down to a hedge. The cottage was some distance away, but every detail was clear in the bright sunlight. A creeping plant clung to the white walls. Smoke trailed from the roof. And in the tiny window, something moved.

The warning voice faded. A final picture grew. Rhoweena crouched at the entrance to the caves of the Old People. And at her side were the leather bags of food and water. Poisoned food and poisoned water. . . .

The thing that had once been Clive Murchison crouched on its haunches, hidden by the bushes, watching the face in the cottage window with unblinking, malevolent eyes.

15

Rosemary parted the curtains of the narrow front room window so that she could watch the car drive away. When it had vanished out of sight she turned to look in the opposite direction, towards the spreading hills. The cloudless sky shaded to a haze, ominous-looking purple where it touched the perspective-flattened, cardboard shapes. The evening was warm, but she shivered as she turned away, letting the lace curtain fall back. For all Harvey was in the kitchen and her uncle upstairs in his room the cottage suddenly seemed empty. She paused at the line of framed pictures that decorated the piano-top, picking up that of the youthful Edward Garvey, looking at it for a few moments then carefully replacing it.

In the kitchen, Harvey was asleep. In the short while since Peter and Dr. Hill had left he had managed to fall fast asleep, hands clasped comfortably over the convexity of his stomach, the soft bubbling of his partly-open mouth the only sound in the room.

Moving quietly so as not to disturb him, Rosemary collected his map and spectacles from the table then carried them over to the Welsh dresser. The map fell open at one of its folds and she could see where a line had been pencilled across the pale green and brown contour markings. She spread it open. The line started from the boundary of the Research Establishment, touched the fringe of Betley Farm and terminated at a circle drawn in the hills. At the centre of the circle the contours grouped closely, forming an elongated oval about the winding blue thread of a stream.

Harvey's voice, coming suddenly, startled her.

"Ordnance Survey, one inch to the mile. How are you at map-reading, Rosemary?"

"Not very good." Re-folding the map she opened a drawer and took out a tablecloth. "I thought you were asleep."

"Asleep?" He sounded offended. "I was thinking." Coming to his feet he went over to the small radio that stood on one of the dresser shelves, reaching across her shoulder to switch it on. While she busied herself laying the table he took out his pipe, tapped the bowl reflectively in the palm of his hand and then used the stem to scratch the side of his face. The radio came to life, filling the room with an intolerable cracking. Harvey turned it off, picked up the map and returned to his seat at the table.

"I was thinking of the things that came into the story." He jerked his shoulder in the general direction of the radio. "The things that must be responsible for that interference. There was the inevitable death-ray, incredible enough forty years ago when the story was written, but not so impossible these days. There was an anti-gravity device and a mind-distorting ray. An equally inevitable force-field, no science fiction story being complete without one. I can recall no mention of a device that would render metal permeable. That must have come later in the narrative." He leaned back. "Products of a fictional technology. An odd sort of reaching into the future by way of the past."

He was silent for a few moments and then he smiled, a smile that was almost the impish grin of a mischievous schoolboy.

"I would give anything to watch the faces of those secretive clever types down at the Establishment if ever they came to clap their eyes on what friend Argred is assembling in his cave."

One idea led to another. He stopped smiling.

"Just supposing," he mused, "that the contents of the cave are recovered intact. It could happen that way. Had you thought about that?"

Engrossed in his flow of ideas he went on, expecting no reply, leaving no interval for one, thinking his thoughts aloud, voicing them in short, unconnected phrases.

"Weapons from another world. . . . Unimaginable, terrifying

148

potency. . . . Devices that could be put to peaceful uses. . . . Anti-gravity—a fortune in that alone. . . . Force-fields. . . . A scientific revolution. . . ."

He was alone in a private world of his own. He leaned back automatically as Rosemary brought knives and forks to the table. When she returned, bread-board and loaf in hand, from the tiny larder, he had finished his monotone diatribe and had opened the map yet again, spectacles askew on his face, poring over it with a new interest.

"How well do you know the hills?" he wanted to know.

She came to stand obligingly at his shoulder. "Not very well, Harvey. The few times I have been up there was quite a while ago, when I was still going to school."

His finger stubbed at the pencilled circle. "This is obviously a gorge of some kind. I was wondering if there are likely to be any caves in it."

She joined him in poring over the map, trying to be helpful but having to admit first to doubt then ignorance. "I'm not sure. I don't really know."

He calculated distances for her benefit. "About a mile and a half from here as the crow flies. Say two miles by the path."

"I'm sure I've never been that far. I remember coming once, with the school on a nature ramble, and we walked quite a distance, but in the other direction."

"And for myself," said Harvey, "I've done very little hill-exploring since I've been here. The spirit was very willing, but the flesh exceeding weak. It didn't take me very long to discover climbing to be too strenuous a pastime for one of my years. And I recall thinking to myself during one of my rare excursions that the scenery in this direction"—his finger prodded at the circle—"didn't appear to be particularly inviting. Bleak, rather, and inhospitable-looking."

He leaned back, discovering with some surprise that the table had been laid. "Ah. And what have we on the agenda for tea to-day?"

Rosemary welcomed the change in subject. "Being Friday—fish. Lemon sole."

149

"And very nice too." He removed the map with a flourish. "Is there anything I can do to help? I'm used to this sort of thing."

She smiled at him. "Thank you, Harvey; I don't think there is. Everything's ready. I'll just go and see if Uncle Edward's awake." She paused. "Do you think it will be all right for him to come down? Or should I take a tray up to his room?"

Harvey pushed himself to his feet. "That's something I can do to help my hostess. I'll go and see how he is."

Alone, she finished laying the table, lighted the gas ring under the kettle and lifted down a frying-pan from its hook. There was a comfortable feeling of normality about the performance of everyday tasks. The sound of voices drifted from upstairs. Between the white plastic curtains of the window the hills were a picture painted on glass, calm and peaceful, lacking reality, with not even a hanging cloud to bring them to life. Looking at them, knife poised over loaf, she shivered again, filled with a sudden sense of foreboding.

Footsteps were heavy on the stairs. Harvey came back into the room. She turned expectantly towards him.

"I don't think it would be wise for him to come down," he said, and added hastily: "He's all right, Rosemary—very much alive and kicking." He rubbed the side of his nose. "He was at the window. I think he had been trying to climb out."

She put her hand to her mouth. "Climb out of the window?"

"It's all right. There's no need to worry. It's too narrow to take even his shoulders. And he can't break the glass sufficiently to climb through because of the leaded panes. He told me it was important he went out. I had some little difficulty in closing the door on him."

Rosemary turned unhappily back to the stove where fat spluttered noisily in the pan.

"It would seem," Harvey said conversationally, "that the feeling of compulsion to go up into the hills is getting stronger." He rubbed his nose again. "I wonder if there's any particular reason?"

It was mainly a silent drive back to the surgery. Dr. Hill, relaxed in his seat, didn't open his eyes until, just after they had negotiated the busy traffic in the square, a car came swinging without warning from a side-street, causing Peter to brake with a jerk.

"Asking for trouble," Dr. Hill observed mildly as they moved off again, now in the wake of the offending vehicle. He leaned forward. "Anyone I know? I don't recognise the car. Off on their holidays by the look of it."

"Or else moving house," Peter said dryly. Suitcases and cardboard boxes were piled on the roof of the battered black saloon. A folded perambulator swayed precariously on the boot. Children's faces were pressed against the rear window. All the ingredients of a hectic week or fortnight at some overcrowded seaside resort. Holidays. . . . A thought occurred to him.

"The hills—I don't remember seeing anyone up there. Don't the local people go up there at all? At week-ends—picnics, that sort of thing?"

"One problem we don't have to worry about," said his uncle. "Very few people make their way out there. The Betley Hills are out of the way for one thing. And for another, there's nothing very inviting about them compared with the Milterns—that's the range about a mile south of Padham. That's where the locals make for on their week-end junketings."

They drew up outside the surgery.

"Nice to see the old homestead again," said Dr. Hill, and consulted the dashboard clock. "Quarter to six—you're only fifteen minutes late. I won't come in with you in case Mrs. Charnley spots me and keeps me talking. I want to catch Mrs. Cookson before she finishes for the day." He grimaced wryly. "That's if she does ever finish work. I'll have the car back well in time for your evening visits. And I'll most likely get myself a meal of sorts while I'm out. All right?"

"But are you sure you'll be all right?" Peter asked anxiously.

"Physician, heal thyself." Dr. Hill smiled a little. "There's no point in trying to disguise that I don't feel up to my usual mark. But that's mainly because of my period of enforced inactivity. Don't worry on my account—I intend to take things dead steady and I'm resisting the temptation of seeking solace in my pipe. If it'll make you feel any better I'll let you run the slide-rule over me before we set off for Betley again. That's if there's time." He waved towards the surgery door. "And now you'd better attend to your more deserving cases."

Not in any way reassured, Peter climbed unhappily from the car and watched it drive away before making his way indoors. In the surgery he found there were only three names on the visiting-pad, all regulars and so not particularly urgent. He was reaching for the bell to summon the first patient when Mrs. Charnley brought a cup of tea and a plate of biscuits.

"I heard you come in, Doctor. This will keep you going till you have time for a proper meal."

He thanked her, supplying: "An unusually busy day," in explanation of his lateness, and then pressed the bell before she had time to voice her usual curiosity.

There were more patients than was expected for an evening surgery. He managed to dispose unobtrusively of the tea and biscuits between the comings and goings. Time passed quickly. It was only when the last patient had been dealt with that he glanced at his watch and was startled to find it was quarter past seven. He went along the passage to open the front door. There was no sign of the car. Peter frowned worriedly. His uncle had been away for nearly an hour and a half. He should have been back an hour ago.

The presentiment of something about to happen—the feeling of foreboding that Rosemary had sensed earlier—was steadily and inexplicably increasing, blending with the air of unreality that filled every room of the cottage, bringing in its train an odd impression of urgency. The feeling seemed to have imported itself to Harvey, for he drifted restlessly from kitchen to front-room window, parting the curtains to peer sideways along the lane, returning to the kitchen to pick up a magazine and then lay it down again immediately. He consulted his watch at frequent intervals, clucking impatiently at the still empty lane as the minutes ticked by once seven o'clock had come and gone.

"They'll have to wait until after evening surgery," Rosemary said reasonably as he stumped into the kitchen for the third time in less than ten minutes. "And there may be calls to make afterwards."

Grunting, Harvey subsided heavily into a chair. "They surely can't be rushed off their feet at this time of year." Digging pipe and pouch from his pocket he started ramming tobacco into the bowl.

"Patients"—he brooded—"I've got a headache, Doctor. Headache. . . ." He thrust the pouch away. "And all this going on." He patted his pockets and then rocked backwards in the chair so he could reach to pick up the box of matches by the stove.

"Do you think Mrs. Cookson will be able to help?" Rosemary asked in an attempt to occupy his mind and hers.

He lifted one eyebrow. "Your young man didn't seem particularly enamoured of the idea. But then he wasn't the other times."

"If it wasn't for Mrs. Cookson," she replied defensively, "none of this might have happened."

"The finger that pressed the trigger." Harvey looked at her through a blue mist of tobacco smoke. "At least it did what it was intended to do—get rid of the poltergeist. I think she only hastened the other thing along. I think it would have happened anyway. It must have been boiling up for the best part of a year, ever since the accident. Perhaps, if this hadn't happened, your uncle—" He broke off.

"May have gone completely out of his mind," she finished evenly. "I know—I've thought of that."

"You can regard it as a kind of psychiatric treatment. That's how it goes. . . . Identify and isolate that part of the subconscious responsible for the trouble, bring it to the surface and then get rid of it. That's what happened."

"Except that we haven't got rid of it." Rosemary went to look out of the window again. The sky drew her attention first. The purple haze had deepened and now clouds had appeared, thin black outlines of their shapes against the ominous-looking curtain. Towards the west they were thicker, massed heavily, scarlet-golden rays lancing through gaps with the intensity of search-light beams.

"Another change in the weather," she observed. "It'll probably get dark earlier than usual tonight." Her gaze dropped to the hills. "Harvey!"

The urgency of the exclamation brought him to his feet. "What's the matter?"

She pointed. "I saw something move."

At her elbow he followed the direction of her finger. "I can't see anything."

"It's gone now. It was just behind that line of bushes."

"That's where the path goes. I can't see anything. Are you sure?"

She hesitated, trying to picture it in her mind. "I'm almost sure. . . . But I'd just been looking at the sky. My eyes were dazzled. Something moved. . . ."

He rubbed his chin pensively. "Someone going along the path. Perhaps a solitary hiker. Or a tramp. Which direction?"

Rosemary shook her head. "Not going along—it seemed to move up and down. I couldn't make out a face—just a sort of brownish shape. It came and went so quickly."

"Brownish," he echoed, and was silent for a few moments. Then: "Someone wearing a brown shirt—his back to you—bending down, perhaps tying a shoe-lace." He glanced sideways at her. "Something like that?"

"It could have been." She sounded relieved.

Harvey nodded. "There's one way to find out." He moved towards the back door.

Her eyes widened in alarm. "Harvey—you're not—?"

"It's all right." He slid the gun from his pocket. "Don't forget this. It could be a child out there—a boy scout."

"It was bigger than a child."

"Distances can be deceptive." He opened the door. "Bolt this after me as soon as I've gone. Just to be on the safe side. And don't open up again until you're sure what's on the other side. You'll probably see me coming back, but in any case I'll give my usual knock. You'll be safe enough—and the others will be along at any moment. Are all the windows fastened?"

She nodded unhappily. "I think so. Harvey, do be careful. . . ."

"Trust me." He smiled reassuringly. "You'd better make sure about the windows." He tucked the hand that held the gun inside the front of his jacket. "No point in alarming some innocent passer-by unnecessarily." He seemed to be enjoying the adventure.

When she had closed and bolted the door behind him she re-turned to stand by the window to watch him walk, almost jauntily, across the strip of lawn, through the tiny vegetable garden to disappear behind the bushes that fronted the hedge. He re-appeared on the other side a few minutes later, busily brushing from his shoulders with his free hand the debris of leaves and twigs that had collected during his passage through the hedge. He turned, saw her watching, and waved before setting off across the open ground of the lower slopes, his right elbow tucked closely into his side.

Rosemary put up her hand in reply and then left the window to make a quick tour of the cottage, making sure that every window was closed and fastened. Outside her uncle's room, she stopped to listen. If all had been quiet behind the locked door she would have gone inside to make sure the window was closed, but there were sounds of movement and she turned away, biting her lip, not so much worried that the window might be open, for Harvey had said it was too narrow to take even Uncle Edward's thin shoulders, but worried about the cause of the restless sounds, the compulsion that drove him to go climbing in the hills.

Downstairs again, she spared a few minutes to go into the front room and peer through the window along the lane. It was nearly half past seven, but still there was no sign of the car returning. The emptiness of the lane added itself to the emptiness of the cottage. She went quickly back to the kitchen. The now deserted slopes, the motionless bushes and the desolate, painted hills, augmented the feeling of isolation. She guessed that Harvey had reached the path and was now making his way along it, hidden by the bushes. He had been gone about ten minutes. There was a fairly long stretch of path to be explored. Allow another ten minutes. . . . He would probably come back into sight again at the far end, where the gorse and bracken thinned. She rested her elbows on the draining-board, her chin on her cupped hands. The slow minutes slipped by. Five of them. . . . Ten. . . . Now fifteen. And still nothing moved out there.

At quarter past eight Peter left his post at the now deserted waiting-room window, where he had been watching the road with steadily growing anxiety, and returned to the surgery. Seating himself at the desk he drew the telephone directory towards him. He wondered whether Mrs. Cookson's number would be listed under her own name or that of her Employment Agency. What the devil did she call her tin-pot agency? He didn't know, but he found the number listed under "Cookson Mrs. F. T. Padham Domestic Employment Agency".

"Servants supplied, houses de-poltergeisted," he said aloud, bitterly, giving vent to his feelings. "Damned woman. . . ." He started to violently dial the number. The sound of the front door being opened made him replace the receiver and come quickly to his feet. In the hall, Dr. Hill was sorting out a raincoat from the collection on the hall-stand.

"May turn to rain," he offered in explanation, and at the expression on Peter's face: "I know. I would have rung you from Northampton only all the call-boxes I happened to spot were engaged and I didn't want to waste any more time looking for a vacant one or waiting my turn at any of the others."

Peter stared at the tired, grey face. "Northampton?"

"Our elusive Mrs. Cookson." The other slung the coat over his shoulder and grimaced in the general direction of the nether regions. "I'll tell you about it as we go. Mrs. Charnley. . . . And they'll be wondering what's happened to us at Betley."

"Have you had anything to eat?"

"I stopped for a snack"—impatiently—"I'm all right." Dr. Hill opened the door and stumped down the path.

Peter reached down his own raincoat and then returned to the surgery to collect his case. He put it in the back of the car and then slid behind the wheel alongside his uncle.

"Tried her place in Padham," said Dr. Hill, his eyes closed, as the car moved away. "Told me she had gone to Northampton. Didn't know when she'd be back. Could be as long as a week. Gave me the name of the hotel she usually stays at. Thought I could get to Northampton and back by seven-thirty. Traffic bad, some time finding hotel, she wasn't there when I did find it. Receptionist co-operative. Gave me names of two more where she sometimes stays. No luck with either. Left messages at all three. Took five minutes off for tea and muffins on my way back. A wild goose chase. . . . Wake me up when we get there."

Waiting at the traffic-lights in the square, Peter looked at the time. It was twenty-five past eight. When the lights changed he stepped hard on the accelerator.

The perspective of the hills had become distorted, flattened, the colours made artificial by the lancing, golden-scarlet streamers of the setting sun. It was a scene painted on canvas, the back-drop on a stage. A scene on which nothing moved. The leaden minutes had ticked by with agonising slowness until three-quarters of an hour had dragged by, and still there was no sign of Harvey returning.

Nothing could have happened to him, Rosemary tried to reassure herself. He had the gun. . . . He'd probably explored the bushes and then made his way along the path, just to be certain. He could easily have gone along the exposed ribbon of path towards the bare flank of hill, and then round it, while she had been at the front room window, looking along the lane. But it wasn't like him to stay away so long, knowing that she would be worrying. He had the gun and he had said he knew how to use it. . . . Everything was all right. Another five minutes and he would come walking back towards the cottage. Ten at the outside. . . . She wouldn't look at her watch for another ten minutes. A watched pot never boils. . . . And what was keeping Peter?

On her way back to the front room she fought back a sudden cold shudder of apprehension that left her legs trembling. She steadied herself, her hands against the cool glass of the window. The sun cast long, grotesque tree-shadows across the lane. The fear-ecstasy returned and she closed her eyes and rested her forehead on the glass. Please, when I open my eyes, let the car be coming.

Fear churned, and the sense of foreboding grew, becoming so intense as to be an almost tangible thing. She opened her eyes again, but the lane was still empty. Above her head, footsteps padded restlessly, the only sound in the world—the insistent, nerve-tautening padding of a caged animal.

She would wait just a little longer before returning to the kitchen —if Harvey knocked she would be able to hear him from here—and by then he would be on his way back, coming quickly down the slope. Please, let him be coming back. . . .

The ten minutes were more than up, she was sure of that without having to look at her watch. Another few minutes more to be sure. The shadows had lengthened perceptibly, a dazzling, confusing tracery of black and green that made it difficult to see along the lane.

She was suddenly aware of a change, but it took her a few moments to realise the cause. The footsteps upstairs had stopped. There was a new tenseness to the unexpected silence. She went into the hall. The kitchen door was open and she could see where the sun, flooding the window, splashed vivid, orange-scarlet rectangles across the wall and part of the dresser. As she went along the hall so a shadow moved across the brightness. Relief flooded through her as she came into the kitchen, ready to open to Harvey's familiar knock.

There was no knock. Outside, something rustled, the brittle sound that might be made by feet disturbing dried leaves. But this was summer, not autumn.

And there was a smell. . . . She backed slowly away from the door, relief draining away, apprehension and then fear taking its place. A cloying, disgusting, sickly-sweet smell. . . . Something scraped across the other side of the door. Now her back was against the wall, her hands to her mouth, all the colour drained from her face. Stark terror had taken all the use from her legs. If she had found the courage to go to the window to look outside, her body would have refused to obey.

The scrabbling sound came again and the handle started to turn, slowly, rattling in its socket as if whatever was on the other side was finding difficulty in gripping it. Panels creaked ominously, terrifyingly. Metal grated against metal and wood splintered suddenly, whitely, at bolts and hinges. The door held for a moment then burst open with a crash.

Rosemary had one glimpse of the thing that stood there, swaying, seeming to fill the doorway, blotting out the hills and sky, and then came the darkness of oblivion and she crumpled to the floor.

16

Peter, swinging the car from the smooth surface of the main road to the rough stones of the lane, took the hump-backed bridge without slackening speed, forgetful of the dip on the other side. The sickening violence of the sudden drop brought Dr. Hill awake but still dazed, glancing about him, blinking.

"Sorry about that," Peter apologised. "I was miles away." He watched the farm slip by and then looked sideways. "So Mrs. Cookson's off."

Dr. Hill yawned. "For the time being."

"By the way she seems to be careering about the country it could be some time before she gets in touch."

"Perhaps. Or she may come home tomorrow—for the week-end."

"We can't let this drag on any longer," Peter said stolidly. "Not even a day longer. We've got to do something positive about it. In any case, she was only a shot in the dark."

"Rather more than that," objected the other. "She acted as a catalyst once. There's no reason why she shouldn't be able to do the same again."

"Catalyst. Dressing it up in scientific terms doesn't alter the fact that—"

"Don't get me wrong," Dr. Hill broke in. "I'm no more enamoured of the idea of making use of her specialised talents than you are. And before you remind me of my earlier enthusiasm, let me remind you that we only had a poltergeist to deal with then. If we had known then what we know now we would have tackled the thing very differently. The damage is done. That's all there is to it. Now it's plain common sense that we fight fire with fire."

Peter slowed to take a bend. "But even if she is able to use Edward Garvey as a kind of mental fifth column and get him to tell us where Argred is hiding, we'll still not be much further ahead. We'll still have to find some way of dealing with him."

"Locating his hiding-place is only part of it. She may be able to give us some idea of the workings of his mind. It would be very useful to know what his intentions are."

"I thought we were supposed to know that," Peter said acidly. "Harvey explained in exhaustive detail. Vengeance on the Mind-Healers. You and I undoubtedly qualify for that category. Destruction of the people of the plains. Which includes the rest of the population. A pleasant line in blood-baths."

Dr. Hill lifted a censorious eyebrow. "Sarcasm—if that's what it was—will help very little. Past events point to Argred living the story. His aim will certainly be wholesale destruction. But how does he intend to go about it? What sort of things is he assembling up there? With Mrs. Cookson's help we might be able to find out. It is always a good thing to know as much about the enemy as possible. Even the smaller details. . . . It would be helpful to know something of the change that presumably is taking place in his appearance."

"Perhaps he's growing green scales and a tail." Peter fought the wheel as the car lurched and skidded across a patch of loose rubble. "Or acquiring additional limbs and multi-faceted eyes."

"Either of which is possible," agreed Dr. Hill placidly, "but, I think, improbable. Admittedly the original story was only intended for a juvenile readership, but I think that the author would have used a certain amount of common sense reasoning in developing his narrative. The change he would cause to take place in Argred could be a logical one."

He had forgotten Peter's presence and was thinking aloud.

"One fact to go on—the strange smell that both Crabley and Brownlee remarked. And the dog's behaviour . . . Argred's mind in Murchison's body. Reality clashing with fiction. How long? Tuesday

—four days. And fiction could distort real time. Condensing. . . . Overlapping."

He lapsed into a brooding silence.

"And?" Peter asked after a while.

"Eh?" The other came back to life. "It's not important." He folded his arms. "I believe you said something positive has to be done about our problem. Have you anything in mind?"

Peter braked again, this time to take the last bend before Betley.

"We take a look at Edward Garvey," he said shortly. "If he's in not too bad a shape we take the risk of letting him loose and then following him."

"I rather fancied that was it," Dr. Hill said mildly. "We've already discussed the risks involved. I don't think you appreciate how great they are, both to his body and his mind. But supposing we do take that risk, what then? We make a massed sortie in his wake?"

"No. I go on my own. With Harvey's gun."

"I see. As easy as that. Always assuming a gun would be of any use against whatever you might find, how would you afterwards go about explaining away the body? Even if a change has taken place it still might bear some resemblance to Clive Murchison."

"Who apparently died a natural death."

"Apparently. But whose body would have a bullet-hole in it. Had you thought about that?"

Without replying, Peter brought the car to a skidding halt outside Rosemary's cottage. He had expected that the sound of their arrival would bring her out to meet them, and he was disappointed when the door remained closed. He turned to help the older man from the car. Dr. Hill, climbing out slowly and stiffly, wasn't ready to let the discussion drop. He repeated: "Had you thought about that?"

Peter didn't answer until they had walked up the path and he had rapped on the door.

"A bridge to be crossed when we come to it," he said then.

"If ever we do come to it by that road," Dr. Hill said heavily. "I am firmly against using Edward in the way you suggest. I want to see an end to all this as much as you do. But I'm not prepared to risk sacrificing a man's sanity in the process."

"No." Peter had a more urgent problem to think about. Frowning, he rested his hand on the door. "They must have heard us coming. . . ." He knocked again, this time a fierce tattoo, born of growing anxiety.

The other grimaced at the sound. "They'll have heard that." Stepping back he peered up at the bedroom windows. "No sign of life. . . ."

His throat tight, Peter turned to look in the direction of Harvey's cottage. His companion sounded doubtful. "I suppose they could have gone across there."

Peter went quickly down the path and broke into a run when he reached the lane. The sun had been swallowed by the clouds, had dipped too behind the hills, and the slopes and the valley lay in steadily deepening shadow. His uncle's voice pursued him: "I'll take a look round the back—" and he raised one hand in acknowledgment without turning or slackening his pace, flinging open the gate and racing up the path to hammer furiously on the door. Waiting, something told him that this was futile, that they weren't here, that something had happened. But he still had to make sure. He made his way to the tiny yard at the rear. The back door was locked, all the windows fastened. The place was patently empty.

It was then that anxiety and apprehension hardened into a cold ecstasy of fear. Sweat was suddenly cold on his back and under his arms. His pulse pounded at the back of his throat as he raced back up the lane. He tried to tell himself that there had to be some ordinary rational reason why both cottages were empty. They could have left altogether, left Betley, made their way to Colford—Rosemary had a flat there. But she would have found some way of letting him know. . . .

As he followed the wall of her cottage his feet caught in a tangle of spreading ground-ivy and he stumbled, grazing his hand against the corner of the wall. The back door stood wide open. In the kitchen he shouted: "Rosemary?" waited, shouted again, louder: "Uncle Andrew?" His voice echoed emptily. Then silence. He fought and partially won a battle against rising panic, forcing himself to stand still while he tried to collect himself, tried to think calmly.

And through the usual domestic scent of soap and household disinfectant he found something else, a cloying, alien smell that for all its faintness caught at the back of his throat. For a puzzling moment it was at the same time strange and familiar. And then a picture formed in his mind, and he knew where he had met it before, knew what it was and shuddered violently, uncontrollably, at the new picture it evoked, suddenly understanding—his mind working automatically as he went quickly along the passage to the hall—something of his uncle's talk of fiction blending with reality, why he had calculated the number of days since Murchison's death. For the odour was unmistakable to one who had met it before. It was the sickly-sweet smell of rotting human flesh, the putrefaction of death.

He found Dr. Hill upstairs, lying on the floor, his eyes closed, his head across the threshold of a bedroom, his body sprawled the width of the landing. Peter dropped to his knees alongside the unconscious man. There was a bruise on one temple. The grey face, the blueish tinge to the lips, the fluttering, wavering pulse told their tale. He threw one quick glance inside the bedroom—it was empty—then came to his feet to race back down the stairs, out through the front door to snatch up the case from the back of the car.

Back on the landing again he eased one limp arm out of the jacket, rolled up the shirt sleeve, assembled a hypodermic syringe, plunged the needle through the rubber cap of a phial, expelled air from the hollow needle and selected a vein for the injection. Still kneeling he laid the syringe aside and snatched up his stethoscope. After a few minutes, satisfied that the drug was taking effect, he came to his feet, gathered up the still unconscious man and carried him inside the bedroom to lay him gently on the bed. Then he inspected the bruise. It was the result of a hard knock, but the flesh wasn't broken. He assumed that it had happened when the heart-attack had come and his uncle had collapsed, probably striking his head against the corner of the door. He looked round the room. Edward Garvey's room. Where was the occupant? The fact that he too was missing resurrected and augmented the hope that nothing was wrong, that all three had left the cottage together, obviously seeking some safer place.

Peter checked his patient again. Both pulse and heart were stronger and colour was beginning to tinge the blue-grey features. There was nothing more he could do; now it was only a matter of time. He went downstairs to make a quick tour of the ground floor, ending up in the kitchen where, despite the open door, the evil smell of death still lingered. The place was neat and tidy, there were no obvious signs of a hurried departure. He assembled a picture in his mind, compounded—he realised that—of wishful thinking, but still a picture that matched the facts.

For some reason, Harvey and Rosemary had decided that it was no longer safe to remain in the cottage. They had left, taking Edward Garvey with them. It was possible they had seen or heard something. And after they had gone, the thing that had once been Clive Murchison had found its way into the cottage. It had been here, but only in the kitchen, for nowhere else was the smell evident.

His foot grated on something on the tiles and he bent to see what it was. A screw, with a splinter of wood attached. Closing the door he saw how the bolt had been wrenched away. It was obvious that the door had been burst open from the outside. Oddly, he found nothing alarming in the knowledge. He had already persuaded himself that the occupants had left before the arrival of the intruder.

He glanced at his watch as he returned upstairs. It was nearly quarter past nine. Dr. Hill was still unconscious, but his pulse was stronger again, his colour better. Peter straightened with an expression of relief. It seemed that the attack had not been as bad as he had first feared. He busied himself repacking the case. When he turned from snapping it closed he found his uncle's eyes open and his hands plucking at the disarranged jacket. He went quickly to the bedside.

"That's more like it." He settled the jacket more comfortably. "How do you feel?"

Dr. Hill tried to push himself up against the pillows. Peter put his hands on the struggling shoulders. "Steady. . . . Easy does it."

The other relaxed, leaning back, breathing heavily. For a few moments his eyes were blank and empty, then they became puzzled as he reached up to finger his bruised temple. And then suddenly they were alive, filled with awareness.

"You must have caught your head against the door as you fell,"

Peter told him. "Luckily the flesh isn't broken. It could have been worse. You'll be all right now."

Dr. Hill shook his head, mouthing silently, seeming to be finding trouble in marshalling words. Then: "The smell—"

"I know. I recognise it. We'll talk about that later. As soon as you've got some of your strength back again I'll get you out to the car."

But the other was struggling again, fighting Peter's hands, refusing to allow himself to be pushed down. "Harvey—Rosemary—"

"It's all right," Peter said steadily. "Don't worry. They must have decided it was best to leave. We'll soon find out where they've gone."

"No. . . ." The other shook his head again, this time violently, angrily, wincing, his hand back to the bruise. He drew a deep breath. "No. Not like that. Edward was still here. . . ."

For a moment Peter stared down at him. Then the significance of what he had just heard exploded inside his mind.

"He was still here." Dr. Hill's clenched fist pounded against the side of the bed. "I called to him through the door. Didn't answer. . . . Unlocked the door. Must have been waiting, must have seen us come. . . . Pushed into me, past me. Knocked me off my feet. . . ."

His face a mask, Peter straightened slowly. His mind was starting to function again, trying to encompass the new situation.

"I thought they had all left together," he said in a voice he didn't recognise as his own.

Without realising what he was doing he went to the window, resting his hands on the glass, staring sightlessly down into the dusk-filled lane, struggling to gain mastery over the surging panic that screamed to set him flinging senselessly out of the cottage, out towards the hills.

Behind him, Dr. Hill raised himself, swung his legs to the floor, swayed where he sat, closed his eyes and then fell back exhausted against the pillows.

A new picture in Peter's mind. . . . Edward Garvey locked in his room—Rosemary and Harvey downstairs. . . . The back door bursting open. And then what? Harvey had a gun. Had there been no time for him to use it? There was no sign of a struggle. Argred must have come silently, unexpectedly, catching them unawares.

A new thought lanced into his mind. Edward Garvey. The urgency of his compulsion had seemingly taught him new cunning. Unable to leave to obey it by way of the window, with not enough strength to break open the door, he had awaited the first opportunity that had presented itself. Now, if their suppositions were right, he would be out in the hills, making his way towards Argred's hiding-place. He had left only a short while ago—fifteen minutes at the outside. He couldn't have gone far. In his condition, burdened with his accident-weakened leg, progress could only be slow.

Peter pushed himself upright, swung round and was on his way to the door in the same movement. Half-way across the room he was brought to a sudden halt by a noise from below, a reverberating crash that seemed to rock the cottage by its violence. It had come from the direction of the kitchen, and he knew that it could only be the sound of the back door being flung open.

Strangely, he was conscious of no sense of immediate fear. Instead there was a cold, calm anger that blotted out all other emotions, leaving his mind sharp and clear. Not Edward Garvey returning—free of the cottage he would carry on until he reached Argred, or the end of his strength. Not Rosemary or Harvey. They would have no cause to burst in in that fashion. There was only one thing it could be. . . . It could have been watching their arrival from a distance. Then, as it must have done earlier, it had made its way down the slopes. But this time it would have something more to deal with than a defenceless girl and an old man.

In the doorway Peter turned to look back into the room, holding up one hand in a gesture asking for silence. His uncle, sprawled now across the bed, raised on one elbow, his face, drained of what little colour it had regained, a grey mask of apprehension. Peter's eyes, circling the room, found nothing, not even an ornament, that might serve as a weapon. He went empty-handed into the passage to stand at the head of the stairs, listening intently, hearing no sound of movement from downstairs. It seemed that unless the intruder was deliberately moving silently—and that would be pointless after the violence of his entry—he was making no effort to leave the kitchen.

In the tiny hall, propped in one corner, Peter found a walking-stick. Picking it up he weighed it in his hand, aware of its absurdity, its pathetic futility, but finding it better than nothing and bringing some reassurance by its feel. The door at the end of the passage stood open so that he could see some way into the kitchen. There was no sign of an occupant, and not enough light left to cast a shadow if someone were standing out of sight. Stepping silently, grasping the stick tightly, he moved towards the doorway. It cost him an effort to cross the threshold.

He had been prepared for almost anything other than the scene that met him. But after the first startled moment it was a scene that told its own story. It seemed obvious that Harvey, his strength almost done, had flung himself bodily against the door, that it had crashed open, and then, carried forward by the impetus, he had come staggering into the room to finally collapse. Now he knelt by a chair, almost in an attitude of prayer, one arm across the seat, head pillowed on elbow, the other arm hanging at his side, the hand clutching the gun.

Dropping the stick, Peter went quickly to his side, stooping, setting his hands on the bowed shoulders and raising them. Dirt was smeared across Harvey's forehead, blood trickled thinly from a long scratch down his cheek. His face was haggard, but he was conscious; his eyes were open, but dazed and unseeing.

It cost Peter another effort to hold himself in check, to force himself to speak steadily, realising that in his present condition the old man wouldn't be capable of coping with more than one question at a time. He chose the simpler rather than the important one.

"Where have you been, Harvey?"

The other stared back blankly. Anxiety tightened Peter's grip on the flaccid shoulders, but his voice still remained calm. "Try to remember."

But the colourless eyes remained glazed. Peter relaxed his grip and for the second time that evening ran for his case. In the bedroom, snatching it up, he flung a brief explanation at Dr. Hill.

"It's Harvey—badly shaken but not hurt. He'll be all right."

Back in the kitchen he opened the case, selected a bottle, found a cup, measured some of the contents of the bottle into it and held it to the grey lips. "This will make you feel better. . . ."

Harvey drank automatically, shuddered and pushed the cup aside. His hands under his arm-pits, Peter helped him up, turning him and lowering him to the seat. Then he asked again: "Where have you been?"

The old man drew a long, quivering breath. Returning awareness brightened his eyes but brought apprehension. Looking about him, trying to stand up, he asked: "Where is Rosemary?"

Peter gently held him down. "Try to understand, Harvey. She isn't here. You must tell me what happened."

"What happened. . . ." The other leaned back, lifted his hand and seemed surprised to discover it still clutched the gun. "He didn't take this. . . ." He peered up into Peter's face. "But he wouldn't know what a gun was."

"No," Peter said. "Try to tell me what happened."

"She—Rosemary—saw something on the hills. On the path, she said, behind some bushes. I went to see what it was. I took the gun. . . ." His gaze pleaded for understanding of the action. "I took the gun so I knew I'd be all right. I told her to lock the door, not to open to anyone unless she was sure. I had to go—it might have been a child out there. . . ." He seemed on the verge of tears. "I thought she'd be safe."

An excuse, Peter thought bitterly. An excuse to do something with the gun. A child with a new toy. Playing a game. . . . But would it have made any difference if he had stayed with Rosemary in the cottage? Argred might have come just the same.

"Go on," he said steadily.

"I made my way up to the path." Harvey closed his eyes. "Nothing there. I walked along—nothing at all. Then the smell—" He shuddered. "It's still in my nostrils. He—it must have been waiting, watching. I saw something move out of the corner of my eye." He reached up to feel the back of his neck. "That's all I can remember. The next thing—I was lying on the path with my head in the bushes."

"Sit forward. . . ." Peter delicately felt the stringy flesh at the

168

nape of Harvey's neck. "No flesh broken. Quite a bruise. . . . How long ago was all this?"

"I don't know." Harvey's voice was stronger. He winced. "That hurts. . . . We were getting anxious about you; we expected you about seven. I seem to remember Rosemary saying it was quarter past just before she saw him through the window."

Peter looked at his watch. And now it was twenty past nine. Two hours since Argred had taken her—that's if Argred had come down to the cottage immediately after his attack on Harvey. But why, if he was living the story, hadn't he killed the old man instead of merely stunning him? And if Rosemary was the Rhoweena of the story, why hadn't he disposed of her on the spot instead of carrying her away? There was some hope in the knowledge that he hadn't indulged in indiscriminate killing. But there could be a reason for that. . . . Harvey might be doomed to die with the rest. . . . Rhoweena had used poison to kill Argred. Perhaps, in the story, she had been killed in the same fashion. But supposition was pointless.

Harvey remembered something else.

"Edward!" he cried urgently.

Peter detached the gun from the cramped fingers that had moulded themselves to the butt. "Edward managed to give us the slip."

"He passed me—out there. Some distance away. I tried to call to him. . . . He seemed to be walking in his sleep. If he heard me he took no notice."

"Which way was he going?" Peter moved towards the door. Harvey pointed without replying.

"Uncle Andrew's upstairs," Peter said briefly from the door. "In Edward's room."

He went across the garden, through the bushes, through the hedge and out into the open. Then he started to climb towards the path.

17

The sombre slopes and the valley seemed set apart from the rest of the world, bounded on one hand by the sprawling half-circle hills, fold upon fold, rising like the steps of some monstrous staircase, on the other by the deepening haze that obscured the countryside beyond the stream. The lowering clouds and the mist rising from the water, sending tenuous drifting tentacles across the fields, completed the illusion of a self-contained place of unreality. The sun had some time ago dipped out of sight, but it was still daylight, twilight not far away, dusk hovering, already shadowing the hollows.

There was no sign of Edward Garvey. Peter, reaching the path after a half-running toil up a slope that had been steeper than it had first appeared, went on without pausing to regain his breath. Ahead, the empty path, clearly defined and bordered by clumps of gorse and bracken, snaked its way along the brow of the hill to swing away out of sight behind a massive shoulder of naked rock that jutted fiercely into the purple sky.

A little way along there was a place where the grass on the verge had been flattened, branches broken from the surrounding bushes. Almost certainly the spot where Harvey had been attacked and then spent his two hours of unconsciousness. That seemed a long time. . . . But perhaps it hadn't been that long—it could easily have taken the old man, in his half-stupefied condition—the best part of an hour to stagger back down the slopes to the cottage.

At the rock shoulder the path hung over the valley. Beyond lay a new vista, a new world, but with the path, curving inwards now to follow the new contours, still empty as far as it was visible. He suddenly became aware of the gun, still clutched in his hand, and he slipped it into his jacket pocket where its weight—heavier than he had imagined—bumped uncomfortably against his thigh in time to his step. He slipped his fingers over the butt to steady it. He could remember Harvey saying that it held six bullets. And cleaned and oiled. Ready for use. Always assuming—Uncle Andrew's words, those —that a gun would be of any use against what he might find.

What he might find. . . . Something that was part fiction, part reality. The reality of Murchison's dead body following its natural course of putrefaction, a process perhaps accelerated by fictional condensing of time. And the fiction of Murchison's mind inhabited by another being, something that was only the creation of a story-writer, changing its form at the dictates of that writer. Perhaps a logical change—Uncle Andrew's words again. In the story, Argred's soul—if that was the right word—had been taken from his dying body and set in a new envelope. And from then onwards his mind had been controlled by the Old People. Mind over matter? Peter wondered. The Old People's combined mind controlling the flesh of Argred's—Murchison's flesh? Was that what Uncle Andrew had been driving at?

Beyond the next hill, with another view—even more desolate than the last—unfolded ahead—the still-empty path divided. But it was patently obvious that one way led back down to the valley. Peter took the other direction.

There was a stream to be forded, a wide but shallow flow of water fringed with stunted rushes. There were foot-prints in the soft moist earth of the margin. Peter bent over them. Two were clearly the marks of someone wearing shoes. And by itself, the imprint of a bare foot, long and narrow; human, but deeply indented as if left there by something of more than ordinary human weight. Or by something carrying a burden. His face set, he straightened.

The path started to climb, a rocky trail that turned to lead deeper into the hills. The mist-hazy valley sank out of sight. There was a narrow, enclosed ravine, the path the dried-up staircase of a series of waterfalls. He had to use his hands to pull himself up. Loose shale grated and slipped beneath his feet and larger stones became dislodged to go clattering down, the sound echoing dismally, thrown back by the granite walls.

When he finally reached the top he had his first glimpse of Edward Garvey. The path dipped into yet another valley, shadowed by the fast-gathering dusk, to melt into the pooled mist at the bottom. It reappeared, winding its way up the opposite slope. And almost at the top a grey figure moved slowly, dragging one leg. As Peter started downwards, half-running, half-sliding on the slippery turf, the figure reached the crest and vanished.

There was a second stream to be crossed, deeper and wider than the first, but with the water frothing about the islands of a series of flat-topped stones. Half-way across his foot slipped, he stumbled and was up to his thighs in the ice-cold torrent. His feet found a grip, three staggering steps and he was pulling himself up on to the opposite bank. He went up the new slope without slackening his pace, breathless when he reached the top, finding yet another mist-filled hollow waiting at his feet, but this time with a massive spur of rock beyond. A silhouette against the darkening sky was Garvey, closer now, but dropping out of sight almost immediately.

The path petered out. The latter part of this new climb he had to negotiate on hands and knees, scrabbling desperately to prevent himself sliding backwards, rising to his feet with relief when he reached the summit, a narrow, even plateau of cushions of sparse wiry turf and stunted, wind-tormented bushes. And then, at sight of what lay ahead, he dropped immediately and instinctively back on his heels to crouch behind one of the bushes while he peered down through the almost leafless branches.

The deep, unexpected gorge, bounded by towering, menacing granite walls, was an alien landscape, a nightmare of grotesquely-piled boulders and dark, foaming pools. He saw where the water gushed from some aperture high in the rock strata. He noticed, almost disinterestedly, the strange metal and wire construction that projected, gleaming dully in the half-light of dusk, from one of the pools. For a few moments the muted thunder of the cascades was the only sound. Then came the slither and rattle of loose stones. Peter raised himself, craning forwards.

Immediately below, on the rubble at the foot of the almost precipitous slope, Edward Garvey was straightening from a crouch, steadying himself with one hand on a boulder, the other pressed tightly against his thigh, coming upright, staring across the floor of the gorge towards the opposite wall. The thing that stood there, a brown statue outlined against an eerie, inexplicable blue haze, bore no resemblance to the Clive Murchison Peter remembered. It seemed taller, but that could have been an illusion of the dusk and the flickering light. Or it could have been because it was near-naked, only a strip of some blue cloth bound about the loins. Even though Peter had tried to imagine what it would look like, had built up a mental picture—and even though that picture wasn't far removed from the truth, he was still shocked by what he saw, horror setting cold fingers at the base of his spine, bristling the hair at the nape of his neck, temporarily over-riding his fears for Rosemary's safety.

The product of reality conflicting with fiction. The stark reality of Murchison's dead body. The fiction of the transformation that, to achieve its purpose, had distorted time, compressing perhaps four weeks into as many days, rotting the flesh, decomposing it to make way for what had to take its place.

The head was hairless, the flesh—what had once been flesh—drawn tightly over the naked skull, gleaming dully like polished brown leather. The face—what had once been a face—was dead, the cheeks hollowed, chin and nose grotesquely elongated, only the deeply sunken eyes alive, glittering points in dark pools. And the body—bones—nothing more than the skeletal shape it seemed—encased in that same dried, brittle brown parchment as the head. The fiction of a living mummy. . . .

The anticipated logical progression of the story. . . . The fiction of the eternal lines of mummies in the Place of the Dead. The souls —the life-essences of the Old People had taken up residence in machines. They had preserved, mummified their discarded bodies. Murchison had become Argred the Freeman, and Argred had become part of the Old People. His mind had become one with their combined mind. And then the fiction of mind over matter, the combined mind changing the matter of his body, making it, like the bodies in the Place of the Dead, ageless, eternal, indestructible.

Indestructible. . . . What makes you think a gun would be of any use against whatever you might find? His face set grimly, Peter slid the gun from his pocket. A slither and rattle of stones was Edward Garvey moving, limping, dragging one leg, his hand still held to his thigh. The angle of the slope and the insecure foothold impelled him sideways and downwards in the direction of the stream, his progress laboured and crab-like. Peter's gaze swung back to the far side of the gorge.

The thing was also moving, lurching rather than walking, the feet coming down with a kind of mechanical deliberation, moving away from the haze of blue light so that now Peter was able to see how it framed and seemed to have its origin in a narrow cleft in the rock. A cleft that must be the entrance to a cave. Argred's workshop—the place to which he had brought the stolen equipment. And the place —Peter leaned forward, eyes narrowed—to which he had brought Rosemary.

His gaze, turning back to the slow-moving, inhuman brown shape, discovered something else. He saw that one of the hands that hung at its side—even from this distance, the brown parchment sticks of fingers long and talon-curved—held some kind of apparatus, shapeless and incomprehensible, but glinting metallically, almost certainly some kind of weapon.

Garvey's stumbling progress had taken him to the verge of the stream, and now he was limping steadily, step by step over the comparatively even ground, moving with the deliberate gait of someone under hypnosis. And the thing was clearly coming to meet him. As it came nearer Peter could see how some kind of tubular arrangement, almost the elongated lens-turret of a camera, protruded from the weapon it still carried at its side. Raising himself from the crouching position he dropped to one knee, steadying himself, swinging the barrel to cover the oncoming figure, his finger curled automatically round the trigger.

And then, his mind suddenly racing, he relaxed his grip. As yet the thing had shown no signs of aggression. If anything, its steady, sleep-walking progress towards Garvey seemed activated more by curiosity than hostility. But each step took it a little further from the cave. There was still quite a distance to go before it came face to face with Garvey. It was impossible to anticipate what might happen then. So which was the more important, to try to protect Garvey—and was protection possible?—or try to reach the cave and find Rosemary?

It was something more than the intensity of his feelings for Rosemary's safety as compared with those for her uncle that guided him to his decision. There was a vague instinctive reasoning—but with no time in which to try to analyse it—that told him Garvey was best left to his own devices. He estimated distances. The thing had reached the water's edge. At its steady, hypnotic pace it would be a few minutes before it reached Garvey. How far from where he crouched to the entrance to the cave? Not more than a couple of hundred yards, but down a steep, treacherous slope and then across terraces of loose scree. He wondered how far he would be able to get before his presence was noticed. There was one way to find out.

Still crouching he turned and went backwards over the brink, digging in his toes to obtain solid footholds. Holding the gun in one hand, using the other to steady himself, he went down the slope as if climbing down a ladder.

Half-way down he slipped, but managed to grasp a projection of rock. The clatter of the few displaced pebbles was too faint a sound to carry far. He reached the bottom unobserved. Without pausing, crouching still, he backed upwards across the scree until he felt the hard granite wall on his shoulders. There was comfort of a kind in its feel, the hope that, blending into its mottled, striated background he would stand more chance of remaining undetected.

He fought the panic-urge to hurry. A few cautious steps at a time, then a momentary pause while he selected the next solid-looking footholds. Then his eyes back again on the strange tableau below, the slow-moving figures, only a short distance separating them now, moving towards each other as if drawn by some strange compulsion.

When he drew level and passed them they were only a few scant yards apart. And sparing a moment to glance ahead he estimated that less than fifty feet separated him from the blue-hazed cleft. But that glance brought disaster. His foot came down on a slab of granite that rocked beneath his weight and then moved, slithering, grating sideways, throwing him off balance so that his feet slid from

beneath him and he came down in the echoing clamour of a miniature avalanche.

Up until that moment he had been able to retain possession of
himself, to be in full control of his faculties, his mind working
clearly, almost coldly, assessing each move before it was made. Now
that possession was shattered, the overwhelming blind instinct of
self-preservation taking its place. The start of the nightmare. . . .

It took him a few panic-laden moments to recover his balance,
scrabbling desperately on the loose stones to push himself up on his
knees, then on his heels, crouching, ready to make a dash for the
cave. Poised, his body tensed, the pulse pounding in his throat, he
looked down towards the stream. The two figures there were motionless, almost face to face. But while Garvey still stared ahead,
seemingly oblivious to anything but what stood in front of him, the
hideous seamed face of the thing had turned in the direction of
the sound.

For an eternity, it seemed to Peter, the glittering empty eyes in
their sunken pits stared back up at him. And then the shrivelled
brown claw started to move, lifting the instrument it carried, the instrument that surely had to be some kind of weapon.

Automatically, instinctively, he brought up the gun and pressed
the trigger. The shot thunder-crashed deafeningly in the confined
space, the weapon kicking savagely, unexpectedly, throwing the bullet high of its target. He saw, almost disinterestedly, the place where
it struck the opposite wall, the scar that sprang into being, a white
streak against dark granite.

As the echoes died away both claws came to hold the instrument,
the turret glowed and light came lancing from it, but emerging
strangely slowly, it seemed, creeping, gathering intensity as it came
towards him, a beam of fierce, blinding blue-white brilliance with a
coiling rose-pink core.

He threw himself sideways, rolled and found the shelter of a large
boulder. He fired again, this time steadying the barrel against rock,
aiming at the source of the beam, trying to anticipate the recoil. But
even so the gun still jerked. The shot went high, but the bullet
found a target. He saw the point of impact, the sudden black circle
that appeared in the very centre of the parchment chest. The thing

staggered, the weapon swinging, sending the beam raking high across the granite wall, rock glowing redly, hissing and crackling, a scarlet swathe marking the passage of the searing circle of light.

Peter fired again, pressing the trigger as fast as he could, three shots in rapid succession. Again he missed the small target of the light-weapon, but at least one of the bullets, perhaps more, struck home, for the thing staggered again, this time lurching sideways with the impact, but still remaining on its feet, the beam sweeping away, dropping, traversing the entrance to the gorge, leaving in its wake patches of glowing rock and the torches of fiercely-burning bushes.

And as he saw the beam moving away, Peter was on his feet, plunging desperately for the more secure protection of the cave, slipping, sliding on the scree, the acrid tang of smoke in his nostrils. He flung himself bodily into the blue-hazed cleft. And then something gripped his body, blanketing him, holding him firmly, preventing him from going any further, enveloping him in some invisible, stifling force that tingled on the exposed flesh of face and hands. The gun dropped from nerveless fingers to go skating away down the slope. For a long moment the force of his impetus held him against the dancing blue barrier. Then he fell away, half-stunned, to lean, breathless and shaken against the projecting side of the cleft. Defenceless, with no protection, he turned to face the menace of the beam, waiting almost resignedly for it to come launching towards him.

Incredibly, miraculously, the thing was on its knees in front of the still motionless Garvey. It was crouching, its back to Peter—and on the drum-taut brown leather of the back, three black circles that were the places where three bullets had passed right through the body. The ray, uncontrolled, wavered, moving slowly and erratically across the opposite wall, molten rock glowing and spluttering, trickling like lava from a volcano. Smoke drifted heavily through the dusk, heavy serpentine coils that hung in the still air. A pool boiled and steamed after the passage of the searing ray.

The thing toppled slowly on its side so that now it was lying, curled sideways on the ground. For a moment the beam was poised, searchlighted high into the night sky, then it came swooping down as the thing that held the source rolled over on its back, coming to rest on the towering crenated granite folds immediately above the place where water came gushing from the heart of the exposed hill. Static now, it bored into solid rock, first a glowing hollow, then a boiling cavity ringed with blue flame. Lava was a trickle, then a flood, cascading down in scarlet waves towards the floor of the gorge. Steam jetted, hissing, from a myriad of cracks and crannies showing where water boiled in hidden pockets and reservoirs. The gorge was filled with the crackle of flames, the hiss of steam-jets, the ominous cracking of expanding, heat-distorted rock.

And then the beam flicked out of existence. It went, not slowly as it had come, but suddenly, as if it had never existed. And in that same instant—Peter saw the change from the side of his eye—so the blue curtain that had blocked the cleft vanished. He went unhindered into the blackness, feeling his way, groping, one hand guiding along the wall. His foot caught on something so that he stumbled, grazing the side of his face. Recovering, he thought of his cigarette lighter, took it from his pocket, flicked it. The dim, uncertain light showed him a narrow tunnel that twisted out of sight ahead. His first move forwards caused the light to flicker out. He shouted, then: "Rosemary!" and relief was something physical, exploding inside his head, at the sound of her voice answering: "Peter?"—asking a question, as if she could hardly believe her ears. He called again, and now her reply was tremulous with acceptance.

Another snap of the lighter, the flame shielded, took him round the corner. He noticed absently that the thing which must have tripped him was a cable that snaked its way along the floor. Darkness again, and he felt his way along the wall. And then the wall fell away suddenly. He snapped the lighter again, holding its feeble light in front of him. A cave . . . walls only dimly perceptible; an impression of piled shapes, boxes linked by wires; glinting metal and glass constructions . . . incomprehensible shapes; more cables trailing across the ground. And Rosemary coming towards him, a pale ghost out of the darkness beyond the circle of light.

He gathered her into his arms, holding her tightly, sparing a few moments for her to recover from the shock of relief, letting her talk, her voice muffled against his breast, her words broken and disjointed.

"It came to the cottage . . . I must have fainted . . . I woke up in

178

here. . . . There were lights—not dark like now. . . . It wasn't here
. . . I tried to get away. . . . There was something across the
entrance. . . ."

"We'll talk about it afterwards," he told her gently. His arm about
her waist he urged her towards the tunnel, flicking the lighter from
time to time, holding the pin-point of flame in front of him.

And then out into the open again, into the hissing, rumbling in-
ferno of the gorge. To the left, high on the wall, rock still glowed,
lava still surged downwards, steam still jetted ominously from cracks
in the granite strata, the ash-piles of bushes still smouldered. There
was the muted thunder of an invisible avalanche.

It was almost dark, but there was enough light for him to see
through the smoke tendrils that Edward Garvey no longer stood by
the stream. In the few minutes that Peter had been in the cave he
must have made his way back out of the gorge leaving the thing there
alone, a monstrous, still horrifying leather-brown shape, lying curled
on the ground alongside the twisted remains of the light-weapon.

As they came abreast of it, hurrying across the scree, Peter instinctively put his hand to the side of her face, trying to cover her
eyes, warning: "Don't look," and then immediately realising that
it was pointless, that she had already seen it face to face, that it was
too late to prevent it being imprinted on her mind.

Behind them came a sudden explosion as the pressure of boiling
water in some unseen reservoir became too great for the rock con-
fining it. It was followed by the rumble of another avalanche. A flying splinter struck his shoulder and he crouched as he ran, holding
Rosemary tightly to him, trying to shield her with his body. They
were half-way up the slope when the second explosion shook the
night, louder than the first, the ground trembling under their feet. A
boulder flew over their heads to go crashing out of sight into some
valley. And as they reached the crest so the final explosion came,
rending the world with its crashing tumult. Peter dragged Rosemary
to the ground, throwing himself on top of her as debris rained about
them. As the sound died away there came the roar of the resultant
avalanche. The echoes died away. A cloud of dust rose to hang in the
still air. After a while Peter raised himself, came to his feet, stooped
to help Rosemary. It was then he saw—had time to notice—that she

wore a jacket slung over her shoulders, the sleeves dangling emptily. A well-worn, not over-clean black leather jacket. He touched it, knowing where he had seen it before.

"It was here when I woke up in the cave," she explained to the query in his eyes. "He must have put it there while I was asleep."

"It belonged to Murchison," Peter said.

"He didn't harm me at all." She drew the sides together in front of her, clutching them almost protectively. "I think I'd like to keep it on. Until we get home again."

He took her arm in silence. They made their way down towards the path.

18

Afterwards, when he came to look back, Peter found himself only able to remember the rest of that evening vaguely, unable to recall little more than a series of disjointed pictures and fragments of conversation. Only parts of it were clear, the rest the blurred aftermath of a dream.

There was the timeless walk back through the hills. A silent walk. And the first clear picture—coming out into the open with the valley suddenly spreading itself below and the distant twinkling lights of Colford an oddly comforting sight. No sign of Edward Garvey, not until they reached the path above the cottage, with the full moon rising above the trees, flooding the world with cold light. And there was Garvey, at the foot of the slope, walking towards the cottage, walking briskly, barely limping, head up, shoulders back. . . . As they started to follow down the slope he disappeared into the shadows of the garden.

Then Harvey Milton and Uncle Andrew standing in the kitchen, turning at the opening of the door. The first inevitable flurry of questions. Rosemary, taking off the jacket, asking a question of her own.

It seemed that Edward had gone up to his room. On the way he had greeted them cheerfully, smiling, wishing them "Good evening" in the most natural way imaginable, telling them that he had been out for a walk, that he had enjoyed it, that now he was tired and would see them in the morning.

"Just like he'd come back from a quiet stroll," Harvey said, almost resentfully, and then would have launched again into questions and demands but Dr. Hill stopped him, breaking in: "All in good time," —smiling, trying to show he was capable of taking things in his stride, keeping his voice matter-of-fact. "Give them time to collect themselves, get their breath back. . . ."

Rosemary, looking about her and smiling a little, back in her kitchen again, back home. "I think we could all use some coffee."

Peter told them what had happened. With the fragrance of coffee filling the room he took them with him to the gorge. He was surprised at how little there was to tell, how few words it took.

Uncle Andrew nodding. "We heard the explosions. Two, at least. We thought it must be thunder. But we didn't see anything."

And Harvey, quietly triumphant: "I said they were too loud for thunder-claps." And then, unreasonably it seemed to Peter, bemoaning the loss of his gun: "It was the only thing I had to remember him. . . . Sentimental associations. . . ." Shaking his head dolefully. "I wonder if we'll be able to recover it?"

Rosemary bringing cups to the table. And then came the black leather jacket. That was something Peter was able to recall very clearly. Harvey setting down his cup, reaching sideways to lift the jacket from the back of a chair, putting it on the table, spreading it open then glancing up, warily, from under his eyebrows.

"The best thing we can do with this is burn it. Cut it up. Get rid of it in the incinerator. Eh?" And when no one answered, "Just to be on the safe side."

He slipped his hand into one of the pockets, laying its contents on the table. Two crumpled white tubes that were the ruins of two cigarettes. Two creased ten-shilling notes. A dirty slip of folded paper. Harvey unfolded it. "Just rows of figures. Train-times by the look of them." He scooped the things up and stuffed them back into the pocket. Peter, watching, felt resentful, almost angry, at the unnecessary intrusion into the privacy of the few pathetic belongings. There was no need for it—just morbid curiosity. But he kept his feelings to himself. And afterwards he was glad in a way he had remained silent, letting Harvey carry on, for there was something in the other pocket. . . . Something that helped solve a problem that had been worrying him.

A flat, white-metal case. He recognised the shape, realising what it must be. And Dr. Hill, also recognising it, reached across the table to take it from Harvey's fingers, opening it, showing the syringe in its purple-velvet nest. A hypodermic syringe, clearly much used, not properly cleaned.

Peter heard himself saying: "So he was a diabetic after all. That's the answer. . . ."

But Harvey still adhered to his original story, protesting volubly: "He may have been. But that wasn't a coma. He was dead. And be-fore—there was not a trace of acetone on his breath."

"Anyone could be mistaken," Peter said.

But Dr. Hill broke into the embryo argument, shaking his head slowly. "This hasn't been used for insulin." Tucked inside the lid was a wadding of blue paper. A faint dusting of white powder showed when it was straightened out. He touched it with his finger, touched his finger to his mouth.

"Heroin," he said, and then there was a long silence.

A little later he broke up a second argument.

"It doesn't matter how much we talk it won't get us anywhere. It doesn't make any difference. He could have taken an over-dose by accident. He could have deliberately taken his own life. He could equally have easily died from some other, natural cause. We'll never be able to find out, so it's no use talking about it. But by the look of this syringe"—he put it back in the case, slid the case into his pocket —"by the way it's been handled, I would say that his death must have come as—" He broke off, shrugging. "There's no future in that sort of thing."

Then Rosemary prepared the table for a meal. And Harvey coming to his feet to switch on the radio. "Just to make sure—" The sound came through without any interference. He switched it off again, turned to Peter. "Did you manage to get a good look at the things in the cave?"

"No," Peter said.

"And the ray-gun it carried?"

"Only from a distance."

"There's always tomorrow," Dr. Hill said tiredly. "We've all had more than enough for one day."

And it was he who, after supper, suddenly discovered it was well past midnight.

Harvey offered hospitality. "Two bedrooms across at my place, a bed in each. I've become accustomed to sleeping here in the kitchen on an easy chair. Another night won't go amiss."

"I wasn't particularly looking forward to the trip back to Colford," Dr. Hill admitted. "Nor was I looking forward to facing Mrs. Charnley's inquisition. That's something else I would prefer to put aside until tomorrow. Or rather, later today."

And that was almost the last of Peter's recollections of the evening. There was Uncle Andrew protesting—and this had to be after Harvey's offer of hospitality—protesting, mildly at first, then more vehemently: "I'm all right. Don't fuss. It was only a tap on the head. If there was a heart attack, and I very much doubt it, there was nothing to it."

And Harvey, nursing the back of his neck with an air of patient martyrdom: "It'll be some time before I forget this. . . ." And: "I'll sleep better, propped in a chair, with a cushion at the back of my neck."

Only one memory-picture was to remain. Rosemary was upstairs, making sure her uncle was all right. Harvey and Dr. Hill had gone outside, to lean on the gate, Harvey with the expressed intention of "smoking a last pipe before turning in." Adding: "Then I'll see you across the road, let you in and turn down the sheets like a good host."

Left alone in the kitchen Peter went to stand by the window. But the moon had been swallowed by cloud, the night was dark and there was nothing to see. He prowled restlessly into the passage to wait for Rosemary to come back downstairs. The front door stood open.

"—came in useful after all." Harvey's voice, that. "Perhaps we still might be able to get it back. Fired it five times. Three hits. Three holes in its back." There was relish of a kind in his tone. "The bullets must have gone right through. . . ."

And Uncle Andrew's reply. "You can't kill something that's already dead." A pause. "In God's name, what sort of rubbish are you burning in that filthy pipe? It stinks to high heaven." There was no malice in his voice, nor in Harvey's reply. They wrangled happily for a few minutes. Both seemed to have recovered from their misadventures.

184

But Peter made a mental note to keep as strict an eye as possible on both of them. Lighting a cigarette he listened to Harvey returning to his original theme.

"That light-beam. . . . Intriguing. You remember how your nephew described it. Only moving slowly—creeping. Not a laser, would you say?"

"It wouldn't seem so." Uncle Andrew sounded resigned.

"Seeming to creep—," brooded Harvey's voice from the darkness. "Blue-white with a pink core. And very destructive. I recall reading an article in a scientific journal some years ago. About something called 'retarded light'. Only a theory, of course. Light is always slowed down when it passes through any transparent medium, it always returns to its normal speed when it emerges again into the air. But if that slowed-down process could be made permanent, perhaps by using a battery of lenses, some of them fluid-filled, so the article suggested, then all sorts of interesting possibilities can be considered. Light would build up and become heat. Which may be what—"

"Tomorrow," broke in Dr. Hill's voice bleakly, "we can discuss theories of retarded light to your heart's content. All I want to do right now is get to bed."

And that was the end of the conversation. And Rosemary coming downstairs, smiling, saying everything was all right, was the last of the evening's memories.

And next morning. Waking to a room flooded with sunshine. Discovering from his watch that it was nine o'clock. Waking Uncle Andrew; washing and shaving; hurrying across the lane; Rosemary with breakfast cooking. "I was just coming across to give you both a call. . . ."

There was no sign of either Harvey or Edward Garvey.

"They were both up early," she told them. "Over breakfast Uncle Edward said he thought he'd go for a walk. . . ." She smiled at their expressions. "That's just how Harvey looked. He said he'd go with him. And Uncle Edward said it sounded like a good idea. He said his leg felt a lot better, that he was thinking of taking a stroll into Colford and that he'd be glad of the company, of someone to talk to."

"Someone to talk to," echoed Dr. Hill. "Well, well. . . ." Then he looked at his watch, observed that Peter was going to be late for surgery and that he'd best hurry.

Rosemary brought plates to the table.

"And he also told us that he could remember dreaming last night. He said it was all mixed up, but he could remember parts of it quite clearly. He was in a kind of tunnel that seemed familiar, as if he'd been there before, that he was very tired and that his body ached, but he knew he had to keep walking. And he said that I came into it as well. We were having a meal out in the open, a picnic, he said, and I'd brought the food in leather bags. And then he was a child again, having his first hair-cut. That was the first part he remembered when he woke up—sitting on a chair, watching flakes of hair drift to the white sheet round his neck. And he said that while he was shaving it came back to him why the tunnel had seemed familiar. It was part of a story he'd read long ago, when he was very young. He said it was queer how you could dream about something you thought you'd forgotten."

She paused.

"Having his first hair-cut," mused Dr. Hill. Forking bacon he lifted his usual eyebrow in Peter's direction. "Part of some sequence that we don't know about? Or just thrown up by his subconscious for luck?" He looked back at Rosemary. "Anything else?"

She nodded. "Just before he woke up he dreamed he was standing at the side of a road, one he's sure he's never seen before. There was something heavy slung over his shoulder, and he was wearing an odd kind of black leather jacket and tight blue trousers. He was tossing a coin, and then he was crossing the road to wait on the other side. A lorry came along, he put up his hand to stop it, and then he woke up."

"A little of each." Dr. Hill pushed his empty plate away. "Argred, Edward and Murchison." Coming to his feet he looked down at Peter. "We'd best be making a move. There'll be plenty of time later to talk about dreams."

An almost silent drive back to Colford. Dr. Hill vanishing upstairs leaving Peter to offer the first excuse he could think of—an all-night confinement—to Mrs. Charnley. Then the routine of morning surgery, Saturday, the waiting-room full. Dr. Hill disappeared again, after lunch, before Peter set off on his visits. He returned just before tea.

"I took a stroll out to the Research Establishment to have a look at our patient."

"I was going to drop in there on the way to Betley this evening," Peter said.

"I thought you might be. So I saved you the trouble. In any case Brownlee wasn't there—they'd allowed him to return to the bosom of his family. I had quite a long chat with Dawson. He was much more affable, not so cagey. He'd already made his mind up that Brownlee's story was the outcome of his knock on the head, an hallucination, and that he had nothing to do with the thefts. And he has a theory about those. Nothing of importance was taken—'junk' —his word, that. He thinks a former employee must be responsible, someone who made copies of the keys while still working there. They've had the locks changed and passed the matter over to the local police.

"Just for good measure I looked in on Brownlee at his home. He seemed happy enough. He's accepted the hallucination theory and was very chirpy about it. Another loose end tied up."

And then tea was over:

"I think it would be a good idea," Dr. Hill said, "if I were to turn in now. Try to catch up on lost sleep." He yawned loudly. "You can cope with evening surgery?"

"I'll try," Peter said dryly.

"And I don't suppose my company is essential to your visit to your lady-love?"

They were in the surgery.

"I'll cope with that on my own as well," Peter told him. "Take off your jacket," he added in a firm, no-nonsense voice. "And your shirt." He nodded towards the couch. "And make yourself comfortable on that."

"I'd been expecting something like this," the other sighed resignedly. "It isn't the done thing, you know, for a doctor to treat a close relative. Not in the best of circles. . . ."

"Lie down," Peter said.

After evening surgery, as soon as he had ushered out the last patient, he drove out alone to Betley. And found Rosemary alone in the cottage.

"They're both out walking again," she explained after they had greeted each other appropriately. "It's almost as if Uncle Edward is trying to make up for lost time. And Harvey—he seems almost afraid to let him out of his sight."

Peter touched the tip of her nose with his finger. "I'll have to get to know him. It's funny, you know I haven't really met him yet."

She smiled up at him. "There'll be plenty of time for that. And Mother too . . . I had word from the hospital this morning; she'll be coming home on Monday. I've spent most of today getting the place ready for her. Come and see?"

"There's something I've got to do first," he told her soberly. "Before it starts to get dark. Something I'm not looking forward to."

She nodded understandingly. "The cave." And then: "I'll come with you, Peter."

"I don't think that would be a clever thing to do."

She smiled a little tremulously. "Uncle Edward wasn't the only one who had dreams last night."

He hesitated then looked down at her feet. "Have you any stouter shoes than those?"

She pressed his arm. "I'll go and change. One of the things I like about you, Peter, is that you understand without having to have it explained."

It was a pleasant warm evening with a clear pale-blue sky and a gentle breeze. When they reached the first of the two streams he lifted her into his arms to carry her to the other side. They struggled up the staircase of the narrow, echoing ravine. He lifted her across the stepping-stones of the second stream, helped her, his arm about her waist, up the final slope. The acrid tang of charred wood still hung in the air. They came to the plateau on the crest.

The gorge had disappeared. Where there had been the precipitous slope dropping down to the scree terraces, the cascades and pools and the tortuous stream, now there was nothing. Everything was buried under a desolation of rock and rubble, the tumbled debris of the explosions and avalanches. The new floor, a nightmare lunar landscape, reached almost to their feet. Water gushed, frothing as it carved itself a new invisible channel. The body, the cave and its contents, were submerged under tons of granite. Dust would settle, soil wash down from newly-exposed hill-sides. Grass would grow, shrubs and bushes.

Rosemary, her face white, stared in silence. Peter, taking her arm, felt how it trembled and knew that she must be thinking of the nearness of their escape. He searched for something to say, something matter-of-fact that would break the spell.

"A transformation scene to end all transformation scenes. Not what one could call a beauty-spot. But then it never was a tourists' paradise." He turned her round, gently, and left his arm about her shoulders. "We may as well make our way back."

He steadied her down the slope. At the bottom she stopped, turned to look back and then managed a smile.

"Harvey will be disappointed. He talked a lot about the things he thought might be in the cave. I think he had some idea of patenting them and putting them on the market."

He returned her smile. "That's better."

He wanted her to talk about it. The thing couldn't be buried in silence as the rock had buried the body. Before it could be forgotten —if ever it could be forgotten—it would have to be spoken about.

"Even if we had been able to get inside the cave the things there would have been useless. I feel sure of that. Just so much junk, pieces of metal and glass. Like the light-ray and the blue haze that blocked the entrance. They both ceased to exist when he died. They were figments of someone's imagination brought to life. But for only as long as Argred was alive. When he died, everything else that was part of the story died with him."

They were silent until he had carried her back across the stepping-stones. As he set her back on her feet she said: "You didn't kill him, Peter?"

He shook his head, echoing Dr. Hill's words: "You can't kill something that is already dead. But the bullets weren't wasted. They saved me from getting myself killed. And they did something else.

"At the start of all this, Mrs. Cookson was responsible for setting the thing in motion. But I think that what happened was inevitable.

She just nudged the thing into being. Your uncle's mind had become incompatible with his body. It created the disturbances that we first thought due to a poltergeist. Psychogeist would be a better word. A mind-ghost. The ghost of Argred the Freeman seeking a more suitable body. Along came Murchison to provide that body. And along came Mrs. Cookson to provide the key to open the door.

"But no sooner was the thing in its new body when the same problem started to rear its head. Murchison's dead body started to change, following the pattern of the story. The new body became even more untenable than had the original. So the thing set about trying to find its way back. The two parts of your uncle's mind trying to come together again."

"Why he kept trying to go into the hills," Rosemary said.

"And why the thing came down to the cottage."

Peter paused. "At least, I think so. We can only guess at what happened then. But judging from your uncle's dreams last night the being must have been a mixture of Argred, Edward Garvey and Murchison. It would be Edward who came to the cottage. Perhaps he saw you at the same time you saw him through the window. Argred took over, recognising you as Rhoweena. He burst in, you fainted, and then probably Murchison took charge, carrying you back to the cave. He would be the one who put the jacket round your shoulders. Or it could have been your uncle again. Certainly, it must have been the Edward-part that went outside, perhaps sensing that its original body was on the way. The two came face to face, two bodies each containing part of the same mind, each part doing its best to re-unite. I like to think that the three bullets were the deciding factor—the key that re-opened the door."

Peter looked down at her.

"Does all that make sense to you, Rosemary?"

"I think so." She sounded doubtful. "You think that now Uncle Edward has a mixture of Argred and Murchison inside him?"

"Not Argred. He's only part of a dream now. A dream that has been remembered and identified and so—cancelled out. I think there's something of Clive Murchison left. But only a very little—no more than what might rub off one person on another if the two are in close contact for a period of time. A little of his confidence and self-assurance. Which explains your uncle's new attitude."

They came to the path above the cottage. Dusk was falling and the first lights pinpointed the twilight haze of the distant town. And there was a light in one of the cottage windows.

"They're back from their walk," Rosemary said, tucking her arm into his. "Come and be introduced to Uncle Edward."

They made their way down to the cottage.